GUNSMOKE NIGHT

Kyle Hardy rode into Sweetwater Valley with a job to do. Before he could act, however, guns blazed on Main Street and Kyle was pitched into a bitter conflict. On one side was Big Bart Brannigan, cattle baron and ruthless land grabber; on the other, pretty young Verity Tyler, courageously standing by her disabled rancher father. In one tempestuous night, Kyle was framed for murder and faced a howling lynch mob — and the whole hellish set-up came to an explosive climax!

CHAP O'KEEFE

GUNSMOKE NIGHT

Complete and Unabridged

LINFORD
Leicester

First published in Great Britain in 1993 by
Robert Hale Limited
London

First Linford Edition
published 1996
by arrangement with
Robert Hale Limited
London

British Library CIP Data

O'Keefe, Chap
Gunsmoke night.—Large print ed.—
Linford western library
I. Title II. Series
823.914 [F]

ISBN 0–7089–7815–0

Published by
F. A. Thorpe (Publishing) Ltd.
Anstey, Leicestershire

Set by Words & Graphics Ltd.
Anstey, Leicestershire
Printed and bound in Great Britain by
T. J. Press (Padstow) Ltd., Padstow, Cornwall

This book is printed on acid-free paper

1

The Massacre

COMING sundown, a lone rider reined in a handsome black stallion, concealing himself and his mount among the deepening shadows of the cluster of cottonwoods on the slope above and west of the Paynter spread. He was a bulkily built man, beefy, and his well-cut clothes bespoke power and money. He noted the failing light and tugged a heavy gold watch from his vest, frowning. He flipped open the hinged front cover.

"What in damnation's keeping them?" he murmured. "Apaches most never attack by night. Die in the dark and your spirit might get lost on its way to the happy hunting ground, the heathens reckon!" At that ghoulish observation he chuckled, and it was not a pleasant sound, for this was a man whose mirth sprang other than from the heart.

His humourless eyes swept the Paynter property appraisingly. It was a modest enough place. The two main buildings — the ranch-house and the hands' bunkhouse — were clinker-built and surrounded by a spruce-pole fence. But beyond ran rich level grassland, and the river that dissected the broad sweep of the valley made a wide, willow-edged loop within the Paynter boundaries. The evening light gave the whole a certain lush desirability in contrast to the near-bald sides of the mountains that rose sombre, stark and remote in the longer, harsher perspective. In truth, the entire Sweetwater Valley was a cattleman's paradise locked in the broken-fanged jaw of a far rim of jagged scarps and summits, now hulking darkly in their night-time hues of purple and black.

The hidden rider's horse snorted and tossed its black mane impatiently, and the man growled, whether in

2

remonstrance or expression of his own feelings made none too clear, before an eerie cry pierced the oncoming nightfall.

The high-pitched ululation was a sinister, frightening sound. Even the hard-faced watcher in the cottonwoods felt the blood curdle in his veins, and he was in a position to imagine the man who was making it, cupping his lips with a hand to produce the distinctive, quavering war-cry of the dreaded Apache Indians. Then the saliva gathered in his mouth and he swallowed in greedy anticipation as he saw a line of horsemen sneaking rapidly through the willow-shaded cover of the river-bank downstream from the Paynter corral.

There was a score of them on rangy ponies. The golden light was insufficient to show perfect detail but the last rays of the sinking sun glistened off oiled bodies, painted with hideous markings, and struck the bright metal of lances and tomahawks, spears and carbines.

The man lurking in the cottonwood copse grinned appreciatively. "Reckon there ain't nothing them Paynters can do about this 'cept mebbe shoot themselves first to get it over quick!" he told himself. He stuck a black cheroot between his lips, struck a lucifer to light it and settled down to watch the promised slaughter.

Other spines shivered too, at the sound of the twice-repeated Apache war-cry. In the ranchhouse, Betty Paynter's hand trembled so violently as she lit an oil lamp that the taper was abruptly extinguished. "Dave!" she screamed.

Her husband jumped to his feet at the table, his dropped cutlery clattering on to his enamel plate. "Injuns!" he gasped. "I don't believe it . . . we've had no trouble in this territory since the army moved 'em into the reservation."

Across the scrubbed board from him the rancher's five-year-old son's big scared eyes shone at him from a face bloodless-white. "Pa!" he blurted.

"They won't hurt us, will they?"

The small family rushed as one to the windows, eyes probing the tricky half-light. Outside, hands alerted by the same dire sounds had rushed into the yard from the bunkhouse and the smaller wash-house and cookhouse that adjoined.

"Get back inside, you damn' fools!" Dave Paynter bawled. "Put up the shutters, get every gun ready and loaded!"

Betty needed no more urging than that. She lifted rifles from racks and wall hooks and piled them with boxes of shells on the parlour table while her husband closed shutters and bolted and barred doors.

Paynter's jaw jutted grimly as he squinted through a vertical wall-loop into the quickly gathering dusk, scanning the aspens and willows marking the ridge that sloped down on its other side to the winding creek. The wall-loop, just to the side of the window, hadn't been used like this since

5

the days when the resentful Apache had raided pioneers' newly established homes. Paynter levered shells into the breech of his Winchester with nervous fingers.

He made out half a dozen mounted, bare-torsoed silhouettes — braves, shifting through the stillness of the trees with furtive intent. He blasphemed, uncommon for him in front of wife and child. "Must be a bunch of renegades," he opined, and sent off three rapid snap-shots cracking in their direction.

At that the raiders broke cover. More fire sped in the direction of the pounding hoofbeats, winging from the bunkhouse which Paynter's five crew and a Chinese cook had chosen for their refuge. But the slugs were apparently wasted.

The attackers, a string of advancing shadows, wheeled wraithlike around the fenced cluster of buildings, unerringly seeking out the defenders' blind spots as though the place was known to them.

After the raiders' sudden advance, a tense silence descended, except for the ever-present whirr of the cicadas.

"Have we scared them off, Pa?" Paynter's small boy asked anxiously.

"Merciful heaven, what are they going to do to us?" his mother sobbed wretchedly.

They were to know soon enough. Their tormentors had no intention of tasting the Paynters' lead. There were more cunning ways to achieve their ends. The first the ranchers knew about them was a whistling in the air and a thud on the roof shingles. It was followed almost immediately by a singeing smell.

"Fire arrows, by God!" Paynter snapped grimly. "The varmints mean to smoke us out!"

Betty screamed as two more projectiles crashed into the ranch-house and an ominous flickering lit up the yard outside, sending grotesque patterns leaping across the darkened walls inside.

7

Within the first minute acrid smoke started to seep into the room and Paynter knew they had to get out quickly or be roasted alive amidst the burning timbers of their doomed home.

Paynter rushed to unbar the door as his son started to cough and cry. "C'mon, Betty, we'll have to take our only chance and run for it!"

"They'll cut us down," Betty choked. The swirling black smoke caught in her throat and harshened the words.

"Yeah, they aim to do that for sure. But I'll try an' give you and the kid covering fire. Head for the stables an' take the bay gelding. Don't wait to saddle up — ride out bareback as fast as y'can!"

The minute Paynter had the door open, the abrupt access of draught whipped the smouldering house timbers into blazing fury and the trio were forced to make their exit in an unprotected bunch. Before Paynter himself could fire a shot, a carbine flashed and roared in the gloom and he was hit full in the chest. He gave a brief groan of pain, clutched at his reddening shirt, sank down to his knees, then collapsed in an inert heap.

His wife screamed piteously, but the boy whom she had by the hand dragged her forward in his terror, as though instinctively knowing that to dally would seal their fates, too.

They plunged across the yard into billowing clouds of smoke and confusion as the bunkhouse shared the same treatment as the ranch-house, bursting into a fireball. More shots were fired. Curses and shrill cries were rent from the hapless ranch-hands.

Her skirts lifted almost to her knees and her hair in disarray, streaming loose almost to her waist, Betty Paynter fled for her life.

Suddenly two half-naked marauders came for Betty and the child, cutting off their path to the stables. The woman gasped and twisted in a frantic bid to escape, but a hand like a claw fastened and wound itself into her long hair. "Run, Johnny, run!" she urged desperately as the boy's hand was wrenched from her grasp.

She was flung in an undignified heap to the dust of the yard, horrified and revolted by knowing what was to be her lot. Coarse glee punctuated the grunts of her assailants as they ripped off the braided sleeves and bodice and the full, long pleated skirt of her grey dress. Then they tore at her feminine underthings till her soft flesh was exposed to the chill of the air and the abrasion of the dirt.

The tears were blinding her eyes and the sobs of terror rasping in her throat. But mercifully they were hasty in their lust. It was only as naked flesh invasively joined hers that she realised the incredible truth, giving a second import to the ghastly groan that wrenched itself from her ravished body. Almost at once the panting man on top of her, recognising what she knew, seized up his discarded gun and blasted an instantly fatal shot point-blank into her shuddering breast.

The watcher in the stand of cottonwood saw it all. From his elevated vantage point between the old grey trunks he observed the scuttling figures, foreshortened by the height. The animal passion rose in him as he saw the fleeing woman stripped and violated; his palms were gripping moistly on the stallion's reins when that single shot ended her life. Between his cruel lips the cheroot was damp and forgotten until it burned low and died. Then he spat out the butt and rode down smiling crookedly to meet the departing victors from the scene of the carnage.

Only one person was allowed to escape the slaying of the Paynters and their crew. And he, though he could not know it, was not spared out of any feelings of mercy, but out of cold calculation.

On orphaned little Johnny Paynter, when he could finally summon the courage to emerge from hiding in a clump of sage close to the low-banked river, would fall the awful duty of telling the gruesome tale of massacre by a bloodthirsty bunch of renegade Indians.

* * *

Kyle Hardy rode into Sweetwater Springs at noon, his grey eyes narrowed against the hot, midday sun. He was dust-covered and running with sweat; his sorrel mare likewise. The externals had him marked for the drifting kind. A saddle-bum, some might judge, moseying around without a care, his clothes old and worn, as though the wearer had seen better days. The shirt was sun-bleached, with many a tear, and the jeans made from homespun cloth worn threadbare at the knees.

But the less cursory observer would have noted his gaze was weary and grave as his eyes took in this new town. There was a resignation of sorts as he surveyed the usual haphazard sprawl of clapboard, sawlog and adobe baking in the Arizona sun — the single, broad Main Street, the horses at the hitching-rails, their tails swishing lazily at the flies; the grizzled rancher haranguing a storekeeper outside the ironmonger's; the loafers sleeping with their sombreros over their eyes in the shade outside the stage depot.

And down the dusty street the buzz of voices and desultory piano playing from the establishment a paint-peeled red signboard said was the Scarlet Crescent Saloon.

Kyle Hardy's expression held no enthusiasm. Was this straggling little township where he wanted to be? By inclination he was the lone rider of the wilderness trails. Over his thirty-some years he'd been sometime army scout, ranch-hand, wrangler, lumberman, and ridden shotgun on a Concord. Maybe some goal setting was in order. In honesty, it was an overdue bid to put some purpose into his life that had tempted him into taking on the special job that had brought him to Sweetwater Valley.

But now he was here he had his inner doubts as to whether the commitment provided what he really wanted . . .

Kyle drew rein and brought his slow-stepping horse to a halt at a long watertrough which carried the carved inscription: 'Blessed are the meek: for they shall inherit the earth'. He was reflecting upon this message while the sorrel poked her urgent muzzle into the more tangible contents and sucked greedily at the much-earned drink when a raised voice broke in on his solitary thoughts.

"Hey, you! You lookin' for somebody, feller?"

The tone was curt, imperious, and it raised Kyle's hackles as he sensed the demand was made of him and felt the hostility of the speaker's eyes boring at the back of his neck.

He turned to see the person who'd

14

hollered at him. It was a big, thick-set man, fleshily jowled and running to fat in the body. A star was pinned to his sweat-stained shirt. He ambled with a waddling gait across from an alley at the side of the courthouse.

"I don't know you," he growled, staring up at Kyle with hard, piggy eyes. "But I'm the law here. Sheriff Lief Coulter. What's your handle and whadya want?"

"Hardy's the name, Kyle Hardy," the mounted man replied. He strived to keep his voice level and cool, but an edge to his drawl betrayed the steel that lay beneath the craggy charm. He looked relaxed and smiling as he leaned forward and laid his hand in a gentle pat on the sleek red neck of his horse. Yet all the while his grey eyes glittered.

"What yuh doin' here?" Coulter persisted.

Across the street, curiosity was rousing the dozing loafers from their siestas. Kyle regarded the sheriff with only

15

lightly concealed disfavour. "If I'm agoin' to tell the story of my life, mebbe I should get myself down from this saddle."

Coulter stuck his thumbs between his gunbelt and the roll of fat that spilled over it. "Ain't no sense in gettin' uppity with me, feller. Step across to my office," he ordered harshly. "You an' me need to do some talkin'."

Kyle tethered the mare and, only slightly stiffly from long riding, followed the belligerent lawman back down the alley to his barred-windowed office at the back of the stone-built courthouse. "Blessed are the meek . . ." he intoned to himself as he went.

"What's that yuh say?" snapped Sheriff Coulter.

"The Bible," Kyle replied solemnly. "I was practising my text for the day."

"Jest let's stick to straight talkin', mister," Coulter blustered. "Yuh're the second stranger to ride in here in two days. What's your business?"

Kyle shrugged his broad shoulders.

16

"Just driftin' around."

"Well, footloose *hombres* is trouble, an' this here's a town that lives real comf'table without it. I reckon yuh'd better ride on, Hardy."

"If you're orderin' me to quit town, I'm stayin'."

Coulter blinked his disbelief. "We'll see about that. Saddle-bums ain't welcome here, feller. Besides which it seems to me like yuh's already itchin' to start a fight!"

How much more of this uncalled-for hassling should Kyle take? His patience was wearing thin; conversely, he had considerations in this territory other than his personal feelings.

But the exchange was given no chance to turn uglier. Light but urgent footfalls echoed in the alleyway outside. "Sheriff Coulter! Sheriff Coulter!" a woman's anxious voice called.

Coulter's jaw worked irritably. "What in hell . . . ?"

The flabby lawman lurched to his feet behind his desk and Kyle looked

17

round to see a slender shape appear behind the thick, frosted glass pane in the law-office door. Then the door was flung open and the distraught woman burst into the room.

2

Gun Duel on Main Street

THE woman who'd stormed in without so much as a by-your-leave was scarcely more than a girl. In Kyle's abruptly interested eyes, her distress did nothing to mar her fresh beauty. He put her age at about eighteen. She was of slim build and average height with hair the colour of ripe corn and very blue eyes that were wide with dismay beneath nicely arched eyebrows. She wore a plain green blouse above a dark-brown divided skirt and shiny black, knee-length riding boots.

Coulter stared at her stupidly. "Why . . . Miss Verity Tyler! What is this?"

The flush in her cheeks deepened as she saw the sheriff had a visitor. "I'm sorry, Mr Coulter, I didn't realise you had someone with you, but it's dreadfully urgent!"

Kyle raised a lean brown hand. "Don't pay me no mind, ma'am. I got no cause to be occupyin' the sheriffs time."

Coulter glared, but Verity needed no further permission to rush on and state her business. "It's my brother Tom, Mr Coulter. He's gotten himself mixed up in a fight with a stranger in the saloon. A frightful, threatening man in black clothes who says he's going to kill him in a gun duel!"

"By God! Yuh don't say Tom Tyler's gone up against that *hombre* Despard! The loco fool . . . that stranger's a professional gunfighter!"

The girl gasped in horror. "Sheriff, you've got to stop it. My brother can be headstrong and outspoken, but he doesn't deserve to die."

Coulter showed no immediate inclination to budge from the security of his office. He cleared his throat noisily. "Uh, well now, Miss Tyler . . . mebbe yuh'd better tell me *exactly* how this all blew up."

Verity glanced anxiously over her shoulder in the direction of the open door, her smooth brow creasing. Voices could now be heard in the street; the expectant muttering of a gathering crowd. "I don't rightly know, Mr Coulter. I was shopping and heard the ruckus from Zachery's Trading Post. When I came out, some men from the saloon told me Tom and a man called Jules something — "

"This can wait, ma'am!" Kyle broke in commandingly. "The sheriff's gotta get out there if he's to have any say in this business."

Coulter opened his fleshy lips to damn Kyle for his impertinence, but the big stranger and the agitated girl were already heading out the door before he could frame the words. He scrambled in their wake, heedful that his tardiness in accompanying them would not look good to the assembling townsfolk outside.

Kyle strode out of the alley by the

courthouse and shouldered his way through the excited onlookers lining Main Street.

In the centre of the drag two men faced each other. One was a young cowpuncher, not much older than Verity and clearly her brother. He had the same fair curly hair and smoothly tanned skin. His features, like hers, were small and finely proportioned, but on him they didn't quite fit because they gave him an effeminate, petulant cast.

The other man, Jules Despard, was all killer. He was lean and tall — near seven-foot tall — dressed in a black, flat-crowned hat and black frock coat. A lean, gaunt-jawed man with the colourless eyes of a cobra. His six-guns had walnut grips polished dark and smooth with use and were slung low on his thighs, the holsters tied down tightly with leather thongs to his stringy legs. The deadly aura of a seasoned professional hung about him like must from a tomb.

Kyle took in the situation with one glance of his keen grey eyes. "See here, Sheriff, unless you're aiming to do somethin' about it, a man's gonna die in this real quiet town you run," he advised acidly.

Coulter's piggy eyes did their best to boggle. "Ain't no call to tell me my job, feller. What we has to do is figure whether this here's an honest, bona fide gun duel."

"And you best do that after it's been fought, I guess." Kyle infused into his voice such a wealth of subtle contempt that he might have gone straight out and called the lawman a sham and a coward.

"Tom!" Verity cried shrilly. "Drop this nonsense. You're to come back home with me this minute!"

A ripple of titters ran through the crowd, laced with ribald remarks.

"Leave me, Sis," Tom Tyler called back in a clear, carrying voice. "It's what I've gotta do."

The hatchet-faced gunslinger shook

his head uncompromisingly. "Let's get on with it," he rasped in a grating, metallic voice that sent a trickle like ice water down a man's spine. "Hey, Lance . . . count up to three, willya, an' make it loud."

With a sick feeling of dread, Kyle knew it was too late for Coulter to exercise his jurisdiction and intervene, even had the twitchy sheriff felt promptly disposed to do so, which it seemed had been improbable from the start.

And with no authority, and one man against scores, intervention by Kyle himself would be as foolhardy as Tom Tyler's own actions in taking on the professional gunman.

When Despard's sawblade voice cut through the hot still air, a man in his mid-twenties strutted down like a peacock from the bunch on the verandah of the Scarlet Crescent. He wore a wide white sombrero and all his clothes were pricey range dandy stuff: elaborately floral-patterned vest, string tie, hand-made boots with built-up heels to boost his height. A wide belt in hand-tooled leather was buckled round his waist and there were twin holsters to match, displaying white stag-handled shooters with steer heads carved in relief. Fancy batwings chaparejos adorned his legs and silver California spurs glittered and jingled at his heels.

He had even features; Kyle supposed he might even be considered good-looking. But the paleness of his blue eyes and the slackness of his full-lipped mouth hinted at a degeneracy and instability in his character.

The role Despard had assigned him was clearly to his taste. It thrust him into a position of significance. It bestowed the chance to show off in front of the people.

The dude called Lance moved out a bit into the street, so everyone could see him maybe, but not so as to invite any danger he'd be in the line of fire. There was a breathless hush while the sun blazed down on the tense scene from a sky of glaring blue, setting shimmering waves of heat bouncing off the bleached, powdery surface of the street. Then Lance's voice pierced the still air.

"One!"

It was only a second before Lance called again, but it seemed to drag into eternity. Kyle had no doubt who would be the fastest draw. Did *any* of the stupid ghouls who must have set this thing up?

A faint hope flickered that Despard might only shoot to disarm. But it died before Lance uttered a sonorous "Two!" These gunfighters had reputations and softness played no part in their making and keeping.

Frozen with his hands away from his sides like paralysed claws hovering inches over his Colt butts, Despard was cold-eyed and looked utterly ruthless. He was in the crouch of the professional gunfighter, knees slightly bent and feet braced apart.

The intake of breath by the onlookers was audible just before Lance, savouring the single word, called: "Three!"

At Kyle's side Verity gave a tiny stifled scream and buried her face in his shirtfront, stranger though he was.

Despard's twin .45s cleared leather with a greased swiftness that baffled every avid eye. They crashed viciously and flame stabbed from the blue-black muzzles. He shot to kill.

Tom Tyler had pivoted on his heel in the split instant he went for his hardware. If his object was to evade his opponent's fire, the tactic was sadly worse than useless. Despard's slugs slammed into him, accentuating his spin, and his own futile shots went high in the air over the towering false front of the Scarlet Crescent.

For a moment he jerked erect on his toes, then he toppled and fell to the ground where he rolled over like a lifeless rag doll.

A buzz ran through the crowd and it surged forward to view the result of the battle at close quarters, though there could be no doubt that the young cowpoke was dead.

"Oh, my God!" Verity sobbed into Kyle's chest. "I don't believe it. They've murdered him!"

Kyle knew no embarrassment as she clung to him unthinkingly; only a deep, stirring pity and the rising of a savage anger. He made no move to follow the crowd and it felt very natural when he put a comforting arm around Verity's shaking shoulders.

Coulter took no notice of the young woman who had tried to appeal for his help. He lumbered across officiously to where the black-garbed gunhawk was surrounded by an awed mob of saloon patrons, the dude called Lance conspicuous among them.

"Get that corpse to the undertaker's!" Coulter ordered loudly and unfeelingly within Verity's hearing. "Now then, mister, I reckon it's time you got out of my town afore any more trouble brews."

Despard sneered. "I goes when I'm ready," he ground out.

Just for a moment it looked as though the affronted sheriff might make a stand. His face purpled, he swallowed. "What keeps you here, Despard?" he asked.

"That's my business, Sheriff."

Coulter was saved from the situation by his deputy who stepped out of the hubbub that milled in front of the saloon. Deputy Izzy Snyder was a lanky man with a long, scraggy neck and a drooping moustache.

"I was in the saloon and seen it all, Sheriff," he volunteered. "The argument was Tyler's makin' an' the young whelp put up the challenge. It was a fair fight."

Verity heard the claim. It and an inner strength that awakened Kyle's wonder roused her out of her grief. Her pretty, tear-stained face set grimly, she pulled free from his encircling arm and ran over to plant herself firmly in front of the sheriff.

"No way will you take my brother to any undertaker's parlour!" she flared. "He goes back with me to the Diamond-T. And I demand you arrest this — this reptile!"

She had plenty of nerve beneath her young, flustered beauty, Kyle thought admiringly. Despard turned his basilisk eyes on her. "The little lady is distraught," he stated in his harsh, remorseless way.

Coulter looked uncomfortable. "I guess I oughta do somethin'," he growled grudgingly. "How-sumever, the evidence kinda lets this *hombre* out."

Snyder leaned over and spoke in Coulter's ear in a heavy undertone. "Sure does, Sheriff. An' Mr Brannigan might not look too kindly on any fuss."

That seemed to settle the fat man's mind. He waved an arm at the crowd. "C'mon! It's all over. Back off here an' give folks air!"

Verity was shocked. "Mr Coulter, you swallow saloon hearsay as evidence?"

"Waal, Miss Tyler, I guess yuh wouldn't have us say Deputy Snyder was *lyin'*." It was his parting shot.

Verity's glistening blue eyes swept around the spectators as though seeking support. But their taste for vicarious thrills satisfied, they were retreating as a craven pack, Coulter and his smirking deputy shuffling after them. Finally, Verity remembered and turned to the big stranger at her elbow. Despair lent her boldness.

"I'm obviously wasting my time in expecting justice from these unprincipled vermin," she said. "I need assistance to get my brother's body home to our ranch. Will you help me, Mr — "

Kyle lifted his stetson. "The name's Hardy, ma'am. Kyle Hardy. And I'll be only too glad. I figure there's good reason someone needs to do somethin' in your behalf. That feller Coulter ain't fit to wear a star."

Verity gulped. "You're very kind, Mr Hardy. I'm sorry to have to drag you into our troubles."

31

"Ain't no need for apologisin'. Your bereavement is a heavy enough burden for a young woman, let alone havin' to beg support from unfeelin' scum."

He could have said a whole lot more. That something was rotten in this valley he'd known long before he rode into the township of Sweetwater Springs. It was why he was here.

But did what he'd just witnessed — the death of this girl's brother — link up with that business? And if so, how?

Whatever, he was now a less reluctant seeker of the truth. It all had to do with the impression made by a pair of liquid blue eyes, a chin set courageously against circumstances turned suddenly violent and ugly. Verity Tyler excited his admiration. He wanted to know more about the enigma of this moist-eyed but spirited girl; to probe beneath the brave front she was putting up to the world.

To try to even the rough odds she'd pitted herself against.

3

The Diamond-T

THE Tylers had ridden into town from their Diamond-T spread in a buckboard to stock up at Sweetwater Springs' seven shops. Tom had drifted off to the saloon while his sister had been tarrying around a rack of women's dresses.

It was left to Kyle Hardy to lift the boy's pathetic body on to the buckboard and cover it with a red wool blanket he took from his own bedroll. He did it gently, Verity Tyler noticed, but as though he didn't notice her brother's dead weight at all. There was an easy strength in his broad shoulders and powerfully muscled arms.

And when he put a hand under her arm to help her up on to the buckboard herself, the same strength seemed to flow warmly from him into her flesh.

What struck Kyle, meanwhile, was that not one hand was lifted to help him. Various folk looked on curiously, but Kyle couldn't tell whether disapproval or fear kept them at bay. He made no attempt to harangue or quiz them, though he was tempted. That could wait. The experience was upsetting enough for Verity without her lone helper getting himself entangled in some fresh altercation.

But he was riled right enough, deep into his guts.

In a black temper, he hurriedly took the rest of his bedroll, his saddle-bags and warbag into a cheap boarding-house where he booked a bed. "Damn the mean bastards," he fretted to himself.

They cleared town pronto in a swirl of dust, Kyle's sorrel hitched behind the buckboard, himself holding the reins. Verity began to sob, all the more heartrending because it was subdued.

It was eighteen miles of winding trail

to the Diamond-T. They forded several streams in the lush valley, the splash of the water refreshing to Kyle after the alkali dust of higher trails. But they clattered over rocky outcrops, too, dividing the tall grasses of the fertile plains, and Kyle reduced the pace in deference to his passenger and respect for the remains of her brother.

Eventually, the girl's tears ceased. At some point she must have decided the big stranger with the craggy face and measured drawl was a man to be trusted. And she talked, haltingly at first, telling a little of herself and her family.

"Tom is — was a strong-willed lad with a passion for pushing his own views and ambitions," she faltered. "In many ways he seemed younger than me, forever the hasty child of the family."

"Kind of rash, would you say?"

He spoke with a slow, soothing drawl. It was a comforting, reassuring voice, exactly what she needed. "You might," she said. "Impulsive."

"I know less than you, I guess, but taking on Despard was surely reckless," Kyle ventured. The pity in his tone took the sting out of the realistic criticism. "Did he make many enemies?"

"Not really, no. But the people Tom had crossed are very powerful in this territory."

Kyle brooded on this a while as the buckboard rattled on. "Tell me, ma'am, I ain't accustomed to stickin' my bill in, but there was a name I caught the deputy use back there. Did any of your brother's enemies go by the name of Brannigan?"

"Why, yes, the most dangerous of them all!" she exclaimed. You saw him yourself. It was the man who did the counting — Lance Brannigan."

"That fancy dan! A braggart and a weaklin', I'd say."

"But backed by the money and influence of his father, Bart Brannigan."

Kyle couldn't fail to note Verity's earnestness. His eyes narrowed. "Yeah,

I recall . . . A cattleman, ain't he? A big-shot in these parts."

"The biggest. Boss of the Triple-Z. Some reckon he aims to own the whole Sweetwater Valley in time. He cares for nothing except self and fortune . . . plus his precious son, Lance!"

She dropped her blonde head and sighed tremulously. "But I mustn't saddle you with Tom's problems. They're all over now."

Kyle was quiet again for several moments. Then: "If there was anythin' you was wantin' me to know, ma'am, go right ahead an' tell me. It don't cost to listen. How come Tom was up against this Lance Brannigan?"

Beneath her Arizona-bronzed complexion, the colour heightened. "Oh, it was so ridiculous really!"

Kyle said nothing while she swallowed her exasperation, and decided he was a man in whom she wanted to put her trust.

"It was a girl . . . I should say woman. To understand you'd have to know that Lance has been spoilt all his life and has an unfortunate sadistic streak to him; also that Tom was totally idealistic and — well, a mite naïve."

"An' it was over this woman that they had their falling-out?"

She nodded. "Maria Cortazzi works at Emilio Vicente's *Paloma Blanca cantina*. She's a — a dancer." She chose the word carefully as though there might have been others it would have been indelicate to use.

"Lance Brannigan acted like he owned her when he patronised the *cantina*, Tom said. But Maria Cortazzi despised his high-handed ways and once insulted him in front of his father's crew. He was in a drunken rage and planned to whip her, but Tom came to her rescue and tipped Lance into the watertrough. Sobered up, he forgot about Maria's insult, but never about his ducking. He vowed he'd get even. But that's something he could never do in a fair fight."

Kyle frowned. "Things are beginnin'

to make a kinda ugly sense."

Verity sadly confirmed the course his thoughts were taking. "I'm told Jules Despard had been — entertained by Maria. When Tom went into the saloon today, he began making uncomplimentary remarks about her. I believe he was put up to this deliberately by Lance Brannigan." She shivered. "Tom saw red and was apparently easily set up for the gun duel."

Kyle let his breath out in a soft whistle and shook his head. "You could be right. These gunfighter types seldom fight a battle for their own selves. They do it strictly for the *dinero*. And Lance Brannigan didn't exactly look short o'that."

★ ★ ★

Old John Tyler, who ran the Diamond-T spread with the help of his two offspring and two hands, had married late in life. The biggest sorrow of his life was surely that he'd outlived his younger wife, who had died of consumption before the children were grown; ten winters ago to be exact, when Verity was just eight. Since then there had been a gathering of many lesser tribulations, so that his life now seemed a constant trial, too big a job for one man, too much to chew. Partly paralysed one year since by a stroke, he constantly worried what black card Fate would deal his kin next.

"Damn it, I'll have no sparin' me the truth! Spit it out, child!" he cussed when his daughter faced him, her big blue eyes red-rimmed and set to spill and a stranger at her elbow.

He fixed her uncompromisingly with a stare of his own, his right eye boring like a gimlet; the left curiously blank in the frozen half of his skull-like face.

He took the grave news with a rigid calm. Afterwards, when Verity had come to a trembling finish, he clenched a bony fist and thumped the arm of his rocking chair.

"By God! Big Bart Brannigan's behind this, that I'll swear!" he cried, his voice cracking. "My son dead. But we'll not give in, Mr Hardy. We'll *never* give in to the bastard!"

Kyle listened respectfully to the bitter vow. "I take it Bart Brannigan has caused you pain before," he prompted softly.

"He damn well has!" The hawkish glint in his right eye fired up his parchment-skinned face. "Bloody Bart some folks call 'im, an' it ain't no wonder. He's brought hell to this territory, stranger. An' all on account o' losin' a wife, I reckon, which is a cross more than one man has had to bear."

"Pa!" Verity cut in. "We don't know what you're saying for a fact."

"Listen!" the old man hissed. "It all began since Elena Brannigan died giving birth to that no-good Lance. After that, Bart Brannigan had no thought for anythin' 'cept self and fortune. The Triple-Z's two thousand

41

acres wasn't enough for him. So one by one he fixed on buying out his neighbours. He kept on growin' even in the bad times, like '63 an' '66 when cattle prices dropped real low. Yuh know how he did that, stranger?"

Kyle shook his head politely. "I guess he had other means."

"Pshaw!" John Tyler exploded scathingly. "Sure he did — foul means! Like unexplained accidents and fires, stock losses to untraced rustlers an' the like. The Triple-Z holdin' is vast now, built up by tramplin' on and crushin' and ruinin' many smaller men along the ways."

"Couldn't no one stop him, Mr Tyler?"

"Naw, there was just no stoppin' him, he were that hard and ruthless, stranger. Yuh was either for him or agin' him — and the devil take yuh if it was the second. Once he'd made hisself president of the Sweetwater Valley Stockman's Syndicate, he was kinda czar of the county. He got the

Sweetwater Springs township in the palm o' his hand. They's scared o' him now. Even the law is corrupt, I tell yuh."

Kyle nodded. "I saw that for myself."

"It leaves us very badly placed, Mr Hardy," Verity put in quietly. "Bart Brannigan has previously made several insulting offers for our land, and now Tom's gone he's sure to put the pressure on again."

Old John set his mouth obstinately, despite the dead muscles in his left jaw. "Goddamn his lousy hide! The Diamond-T is a small but handsome spread, Hardy, an' we've worked hard to make it so. Brannigan ain't gettin' it for a measly song!"

Kyle recognised the source of the stubborn pride and determination he'd already glimpsed in the rancher's daughter.

A little later, Kyle and Verity went back out into the yard and crossed to the shed where the buckboard was with its grisly burden. She said, "I haven't had much chance to voice my appreciation for your coming back with me like you did, Mr Hardy, and I'm afraid my father is sparing with his thanks."

"No matter, ma'am. The load he has on his mind is a heavy burden."

Two other men were in the shed, an old-timer with a black beard and bowlegs and a younger man whom Kyle noticed had only three fingers on his right hand. Hearing the approaching pair, the men turned, and Verity introduced them.

"This here's our *segundo*, Ned Hammond," Verity said, nodding in the direction of the older man.

"Howdy." Hammond was wary, his watery eyes sizing Kyle up, noting the broad, powerful shoulders and the slim, athlete's waist. Here was a solid, capable man with plenty of good work in him, he assessed, but something in the steely grey eyes gave him cause to think twice. There was a restlessness in those eyes that a man at peace with himself didn't have.

Verity was completing her introductions. "And Steve Ellison makes up the rest of the crew."

Ellison dipped his head self-consciously.

"We ain't much of a team in numbers, Hardy," Hammond said. "And losin' Tom like this is a helluva blow in every way."

"There were more hands once," Verity explained as if feeling guilty. "But that bully Brannigan scared most of them off."

"For a fact!" Hammond agreed. "When they seen the violence what befell them that backed Brannigan's opposition, they lit out." He spat into the dust and wiped his whiskers with the back of a horny hand.

Ellison scowled. "Aw . . . that weren't all. Brannigan and his Syndicate cronies lured away them that was less fussy with higher wages."

"When yuh rides with the Brannigans, yuh sell your soul to the devil!" wheezed Hammond. "Me an' Ellison ain't no account to 'em, I reckon. If'n they made us an offer, it'd be risky to refuse, seein' what happens to fellers thet do. Consider th' rewards o'them that stuck by the Paynters."

Kyle's ears pricked up.

Verity frowned. "The Paynter spread was attacked by renegade Apaches, Ned."

"Sure, thet's what we was led to suppose, an' I ain't meanin' t' step on yore purty toes, Miss Verity, but it was only on the sayso o' Dave an' Betty's boy. The pore li'le dev'l was the only one thet wasn't wiped out, an' he was whisked off back East to his uncle in Virginia right off. Anyways, what's fer sure is thet the executors sold the place off to Brannigan fer less than it were worth."

Verity's face was troubled. "No one knows anything about the Paynter slaying that isn't gossip or rumour," she told Ned firmly. "You mustn't be scared off. Pa and I would be finished if you and Steve left."

Kyle didn't have to do any complicated sums. Two old men, one part paralysed, one younger man kind of diffident, and a girl of eighteen, spunky and pretty but with no real appreciation of her vulnerability . . . the Diamond-T was in deep trouble. No one would bet on its chances of surviving an unscrupulous bid to take it over. Alone, the Tylers wouldn't have a prayer.

He sighed heavily. Everything was stacked against the pair. But was it any of his business? He had other things to pay mind to in Sweetwater Valley.

The least he could do, however, was to help see Tom Tyler decently buried. The kid couldn't deserve less, goddamn fool though he'd been.

Hammond handed him a long-handled shovel and together with Ellison they made their way to a grove of silver beeches that lined a ridge diagonally across from the house, to a spot out of the glaring heat that had been pointed out by Verity. "Much obliged t' yuh," Hammond said.

47

They buried Tom as the sun went down. Old man Tyler, clutching a prayer book, led the proceedings and Verity read some words from a heavy-bound family Bible.

"We therefore commit his body to the ground," John Tyler intoned. "Earth to earth, ashes to ashes, dust to dust; in sure an' certain hope of the Resurrection to eternal life."

"Amen," Kyle murmured along with the others, his bared head bowed.

The men built a mound of stones over the grave and when it was done Verity placed a simple wooden cross as a marker. She herself had sawn the planks and burned the inscription into the wood while Kyle, Hammond and Ellison had been digging.

Afterwards, it was hard for Kyle to pinpoint the moment when the impulse came for him to commit himself. Maybe it was when he lifted his reflective gaze from Tom's grave and found himself looking full into the sad yet hauntingly lovely blue eyes of the dead young man's sister. An unseemly desire came upon him to sweep her into his arms, crush her to him, bury his face in her shiny blonde hair. Instead, he held out his arm to her, to support her back to the house in the path of her father. The two ranch-hands were already helping the old man, who walked with the aid of a stout ash stick.

Kyle said gently, "Don't let this sound like I'm tryin' to step into a dead man's boots, 'cause I know I can't ever fill the place of your brother, but it occurs to me, ma'am, your pa has a vacancy for an extra hand."

"An extra hand!" Verity echoed the words disbelievingly. "Mr Hardy, are you volunteering to ride for the Diamond-T?"

"Sure am."

"Aren't you scared you'd be signing your own death warrant?"

"Waal, if that's the way of it, you surely need all the help you can get," he drawled grimly. "Anyhows, I got the time to spare afore I push on outa the territory."

"I'm sure you'll be very welcome, Mr Hardy, but I don't know that we can pay much for your hire."

"Jest to stay around I'll settle for whatever your pa can afford."

"Why are you doing this?"

Kyle's mouth twisted. "It began with what I saw in town, an' what I've heard since hasn't made it no better. Jest let's say I don't like to see folks pushed around."

Old John was delighted to hear that the Diamond-T had a new recruit. "This makes us doubly in your debt, feller. I just hope yuh don't live to regret it."

Hammond wrung Kyle's hand in his own calloused paw. "Welcome aboard, Hardy. Reckon t'day's brung us no end o'shocks, though this 'un's a diff'rent colour."

But when he'd shown Kyle where to stable his bronc and given him a place in the bunkhouse, the aged foreman shook his head in wonder.

"Sure beats the hell outa me. A well set-up *hombre* like him . . . Once the Brannigans get wind o' this, his life ain't gonna be worth a plugged nickel!"

4

Dark Beauty

KYLE HARDY rode back to Sweetwater Springs that evening to cancel his room at the boarding-house and collect his gear. Before he left the Diamond-T he spent long, patient moments checking and oiling his guns.

He went cautiously at first in the failing light, but when a three-quarter moon rose over the rim of the far mountains, he gave the rested red sorrel her head. The rush of the breeze he made was refreshing, spiced with the scent of flowering sage and yucca.

In town, the boarding-house woman, an obese crone, came down breathlessly to the fusty lobby of her establishment, a shapeless red flannel dressing-gown over her night attire. The rickety swivel chair behind the battered roll-top desk creaked as it received her enormous bulk. "Nothin' wrong with your room, was there?" she challenged wheezily.

"No, ma'am, I got myself a job is all," Kyle informed her politely. "I'll be dossin' down at the Diamond-T."

"Cain't give you a full refund," the gross woman puffed. She pulled a rattling tin cash-box out of the desk. Her eyes glimmered with resentment at the lost business. "Three dollars is a — a booking fee."

It sounded as though the idea had just presented itself to her devious mind, but Kyle wasn't arguing so long as he got his bags and his bedroll.

The woman glowered after him as he left. As the widowed sister of Sheriff Lief Coulter she'd been an especially interested spectator to the dramatic proceedings on Main Street earlier in the day. She'd seen the drifter come to Verity Tyler's aid and ride out with her on the Diamond-T rig. Now, no sooner had Kyle gone than she put on an outdoor cloak and slipped quickly out her back door.

Meanwhile, Kyle took himself across to the *Paloma Blanca cantina*. He could use a drink before he headed back to the ranch and at the *cantina*, he remembered Verity telling him, worked Maria Cortazzi, the so-called dancer alleged to be the cause of the fatal dispute between Tom Tyler and the gunhawk Jules Despard. Maybe he would see her, even ask a few questions if the chance arose.

Horses stood flank to flank at the hitching-rail outside the *Paloma Blanca*, the biggest and brightest spot in town. The half-drunken, loud-mouthed hubbub coming from within told Kyle, even before he shoved through the batwings, that the place was doing brisk business, probably from cowhands who'd ridden in from the spreads surrounding the town and reaching down the valley.

Kyle had barely had time to reach the bar and order a mug of beer than music struck up from a low platform across the smoke-filled room. A swarthy man, immaculate in a frill-fronted shirt and a black Prince Albert, stepped out of the shadows behind the long counter and came up alongside the barkeep. His Mexican accent blended obsequiousness with pride.

"Good evening, *señor*, you ees a stranger, eh, no? And you ees just in time for the special pleasure. Thees ees our showtime and you weell see how I, Emilio Vicente, prepare theengs for your enjoyment."

A break of chords on mandolins and guitar reduced the noise in the heated room to an expectant murmur. A drab curtain was plucked aside behind the Mexican musicians and a young woman came out into the lamplight, all scarlet and black and white. She was a black-haired, bold-eyed beauty with creamy white skin, full red lips and a superb body.

It was clear the men here were crazy about her. They whooped and hollered as she whirled across the *cantina's* dusty floor and flung into a vigorous *fandango*. Her red silk shawl was sent flying, her toes twinkled, castanets clicked between her slim fingers.

Emilio Vicente expressed his enthusiasm as volubly as the others. "Bravo, Maria!" he called. "Bravo!" Then he winked at Kyle. "She ees — what ees eet you *Americanos* say — the one helluva looker, *si*?" he said with a leer.

Silently Kyle agreed that she was attractive enough, with unmistakably sensuous charms. But he suspected her beauty might not stand up under closer inspection, and her shapeliness was of a voluptuous, *pelado* kind. Still, she had her followers here. Probably she gave performances of a more intimate kind for the right *dinero*. It was the unquestioned and unquestioning way with these saloon girls in frontier towns. And she was clearly a cut above the other Mex 'hostesses' who threaded through the crowds with trays of drinks, little averse to the slaps and pinches of the rowdy cowpokes.

A storm of handclapping, whistling and foot stomping greeted the end of Maria's dance. There were cries for an encore, but Maria only flung back her head in a laughing, breathless refusal, stretching the thin white blouse tightly over her heaving full breasts. A way parted for her as she made for the bar and a cooling drink, her brow damp with perspiration.

Kyle watched her passage and noted none of the men dared to take the liberties they were taking with the other girls. He tossed up mentally whether he should ask Vicente to tell him more about his star dancer, and decided against it.

In fact, the *cantina* proprietor could not have told him much. Maria Cortazzi had stepped off the night stage in Sweetwater Springs late one evening some two years ago.

To Emilio Vicente the girl's heritage remained unknown. He merely knew that she was from south of the Border, that she'd brought all her possessions in one small, battered tin trunk, and she'd been looking for work. Any work.

She could dance, she'd told Vicente. He'd taken one look at her ripe body and engaged her on the spot. Ever since, he'd been congratulating himself on the good fortune that had sent her his way. She was worth every dollar he paid her. Furthermore, she handed over a healthy percentage of the money she took from the favoured clientele she comprehensively 'entertained' in her room upstairs at the rate of ten dollars for half an hour or fifty dollars the night. The cash that flowed to Vicente was no chicken-feed.

A barely perceptible tilt of Maria's head and a quick flutter of her long black eyelashes told Kyle she'd sensed his avid attention. She in turn was sizing up the big stranger herself, in a knowing, professional way.

Kyle's grip tightened round his glass and he leaned back against the bar. He had no doubt she could tell him things about this community that Verity, or even her father, would never have guessed at. But the opportunity to make her acquaintance was abruptly postponed.

A familiar figure emerged from the jostle of cowpokes and swaggered into the space beside him at the bar, cutting off the exchange of glances. It was the dandy, Lance Brannigan. A loose-lipped grin hung on his sallow face.

"Howdy, mister, stranger hereabouts?"

Kyle regarded him distastefully. The reek of some strong pomade irritated his nostrils. "If you ain't one yourself, I guess that's kinda obvious."

Pale blue eyes glittered. "No call to get testy, mister. I hear you're planning to stay around a while."

Kyle was not swift enough to mask his surprise. "Who told you that?"

"I hear it right off from the sheriff's office. Deputy Snyder no less. Seems like the law here's gotten an interest in you." He flicked unseen dust from his ornately buttoned sleeve. You or them cock-eyed foolish Tylers you've taken up with."

"What's it to you?" Kyle gritted.

"Don't take no offence, stranger, but it crosses my mind you're backing a loser. Mebbe you could find yourself needing more useful friends."

"Speak plain, feller!" Kyle rapped. He thumped his empty mug down on the bar.

Brannigan swallowed, his Adam's apple bulging in his throat. Two hard-faced waddies slipped up and ranked themselves behind him, glowering at Kyle intimidatingly.

"Give this man a fresh bottle, barkeep!" Lance ordered. "I aim to keep this conversation friendly like. See here, mister, me and my friends were telling Deputy Snyder we could offer you a better deal at the Triple-Z . . . like fifty a month and grub and a clean nose with the law, no questions."

Kyle looked coldly at him. "I don't

want none of your liquor or friendship, an' an honest man don't quit a job on the same day he takes it."

Lance blinked at the brusque reply. The spoilt son of Big Bart Brannigan wasn't used to taking no for an answer. For too long, everything — fancy clothes, booze, women — had been his for the asking. His reaction was to up the bidding. "Sixty a month then. That's mighty fine *dinero* for a drifting cowpuncher."

"I dare say," Kyle said roughly. "But you've already had my answer an' I'm stickin' to it come hell or high water."

Lance checked his anger, hating to think he was losing face in front of his father's two toughs. His shrewd eyes had been on Kyle for several moments before he'd made his play. Now he threw a new card.

He nodded toward the voluptuous Maria. "Nice pickings, huh?" he murmured conspiratorially. "What do you say to us putting you in her bed for the night, just to sweeten the deal?"

Kyle looked at him with contempt. "I'm flattered to death," he scorned, backing off. "Before I need a range cissy's help in *that* direction, the Rio Grande is gonna be frozen over."

The pair were suddenly aware that much of the commotion in the room had stilled and that eyes were turning, intrigued, in their direction. Some recognised the stranger who'd stepped in to help Verity Tyler after her brother had been killed that afternoon.

"Why, you stinking trail louse!" Lance spat, hectic splotches of colour rising in his sallow cheeks. "No sonofabitch gives *me* lip!"

"Is that so?" Kyle said witheringly. "Waal, mebbe you'd better do somethin' about it, 'cause I reckon amongst them peacock colours o' your'n, there's a yellow streak a foot wide down your back!"

A heavy silence fell over the gathering. The quietened roisterers stared with disbelieving eyes. Along the bar, Maria put down her glass as if it was in danger of spontaneously shattering. A tongue flicked over her full red lips.

Then a voice from out of the swirling smoke haze at the back of the room yelled, "Hit him, Lance! Larn the interferin' bastard a lesson!"

Lance knew he'd been trapped by his own fighting talk. "You betcha!" he snarled, and without preliminaries landed the first punch full in Kyle's face.

Kyle staggered but stayed on his feet. It looked to the hushed audience like it had hurt the younker's fist more than the big stranger's craggy countenance.

Kyle swiftly figured the rakish Brannigan didn't have the weight to put him down with one blow. He put up his own fists defensively and weaved warily, waiting for a further rush from the furious dude. He brushed the water from his narrowed eyes with his sleeve.

The crowd had drawn itself into a half-circle round the combatants, the other side formed by the counter. It broke into an excited gabble as blood released by the first rude punch started to trickle belatedly from Kyle's nose.

"Go on, Lance!" someone shouted. "Kill 'm! He's run out of sand already. Look at it, will yuh? He's scared sick an' backin' off!"

There were several similar cries and Lance was emboldened to make a second vicious stab for Kyle's nose with his beringed right fist.

Kyle was ready for him. He sidestepped the blow and drove a quick, short-arm jab into the embroidered vest that covered Lance's midriff.

The wind rushed out of Lance's lungs; he staggered, rasping in fresh breath in the close atmosphere of the *cantina*.

Kyle eyed him pityingly. "You wanna change your mind, skunk?"

"The hell with that!" Lance whispered hoarsely, and flung himself forward again, fists flailing.

Kyle fought back coolly. He hit

him upstairs, then downstairs. Every time his mighty fist made contact, Lance's pale eyes boggled with pain. And Kyle knew that with each blow struck back at him, his impassioned opponent was mostly wearing himself down. He wondered when the kid had last had to fight a battle of his own, if ever.

Lance tried the odd dirty trick; nothing was barred, it seemed, in this rough-and-tumble. The first foul was a knee to the crotch. Then, as Kyle doubled up with a gasp, Lance aimed his fancy leather boot at his opponent's chin.

Those who worked for the Brannigans, sold things to them, or otherwise grew fat by their sufferance, growled animal-like approval.

But Kyle ducked to one side and the vicious toe missed its mark, throwing Lance off balance and leaving him open to a hefty clip on the jaw that crunched his teeth together.

The fight was too unscientific to

last long. Kyle didn't have to hit the young Brannigan many more times, and when he did his punches packed telling strength. The power of his corded forearm muscles and sinewy body was behind each blow.

Battered, his string tie adrift and his fine silk shirt ripped, Lance swung a punch groggily, failed to connect and tripped over his own feet. He fell. His brow struck the brass rail at the bar front and he was out to the world, a senseless heap.

Kyle saw the next treacherous move out of the corner of his eye. One of the two Triple-Z toughs who'd stood by their boss's son went for a gun.

5

Upstairs at the Paloma Blanca

THE gunnie's six-shooter was half out of his holster when a Colt seemed to spin into Kyle Hardy's hand from his right thigh and spat red lightning. The Triple-Z man triggered almost instantaneously and the roar of two shots reverberated through the *cantina*, battering eardrums.

The second bullet ploughed harmlessly into the floor, kicking up the sawdust. But the first, Kyle's, ripped into flesh and bone. The ponderous slam of the .45 slug shattered the trigger-happy cowpoke's wrist and he let out a giant howl of fury and pain.

The acrid whiff of gunsmoke joined the blue-grey layers that hung over the room.

"Anyone else draws an' I shoot to kill," Kyle announced. The terse threat was still sinking into the dumbstruck onlookers when Sheriff Lief Coulter waddled rapidly through the batwings followed by his deputy, Izzy Snyder.

"Yuh mighta known it, Sheriff," Snyder said, his head thrust forward on his scraggy neck. "It's that goddamn saddle-bum. He's still got his iron in his hand."

Coulter's eyes took swift stock. Alarm brightened his piggy eyes when he saw the dishevelled son of the territory's richest rancher pulling himself groggily to his feet. Almost as bad, a tough he healthily respected as one of the same rancher's top hands was clutching a blood-dripping arm, his unlovely features contorted with pain and hate.

"This does it, Hardy. It would of had to be you," he said harshly. "Throw down that hardware an' come along with me. Yuh can cool down in the calaboose, while we figures out what to do with yuh!"

"You're readin' it wrong, Sheriff," Hardy said, making no attempt to drop his Colt but simply holstering it. "These fellers set about me. I certainly didn't go for my gun first. That was this *hombre* here."

Coulter looked uneasy and shuffled his feet. Snyder, who'd been tugging his drooping moustache reflectively, chipped in. "Mebbe we should inquire as to whether there was any *witnesses* to that, Sheriff," he suggested heavily.

"Dead right, Deputy," Coulter agreed. He looked eagerly round the ring of onlookers, most of them hands from the Triple-Z and other spreads that owed allegiance to the influential Sweetwater Valley Stockman's Syndicate. "Any of you fellers see Hoffman go for his gun first?"

No one spoke.

"Waal, looks like yuh earned yourself a spell in jail, Hardy," Coulter said. A tight smile of satisfaction took up some slack from his flabby jowls.

"He's sewed hisself up with this one,

Sheriff," Snyder affirmed.

"So that's the way of it, eh?" Kyle asked, his grey eyes sweeping the scene and despising the cowardice he saw. An ironic smile creased his craggy bronze features.

"No, it is not."

An audible gasp was raised by the warm husky voice that spoke from down the bar. The dancer, Maria Cortazzi, stepped forward into the open space before Coulter.

"I see it all from where I stand and it is my *obligation* to speak." Her dark eyes gleamed and her head was held at a proud tilt.

Coulter gulped. "Are you backin' up this coyote's yarn?"

"*Si*, it is as he say, Señor Coulter. The kid Brannigan fight him with fists, but he lose and the — how you say? — wet-nurse Hoffman draw his gun first."

Lance Brannigan yapped an indignant oath. His senses were slowly returning. But no one took any notice of him.

70

All eyes were glued to the dark beauty in a way that transcended her normal fascination. Despite her station, something in her unknown ancestry lent an air of aristocratic authority to her bearing that was more than enough to faze the malleable sheriff.

Overawed and embarrassed by her intervention, he lost his precariously held initiative.

"Waal, I dunno . . . " he stumbled, red-faced.

"It is the fair play, *señor*. You cannot arrest him without these other men also, and Hoffman he must go to the doctor *pronto*. So the stranger, who I will testify is innocent of this thing, he must be free as well."

Kyle smiled at her. "I'm real glad to have you speak for me, ma'am," he drawled pleasantly. "It was gettin' to kinda worry me I might have to go against the sheriff here. But I figure he's gonna have to do like you say."

Kyle knew he was pulling some bluff, but he could sense opinion within the

71

crowded cantina was being swayed if not in his direction, at least to a more neutral position. The magic of the sexy Maria's charisma had them spellbound.

The woman furthered his new advantage. "You were within your rights, *señor*, a man has to protect himself," she told him. "This is a free and glorious country this America, is it not?" The last words were subtly delivered to the room at large.

A murmur of assent went up. Coulter found himself at a loss to challenge her, and various onlookers started to drift away, some no doubt seeking safer, less contentious surroundings in quieter water holes, like the Scarlet Crescent saloon.

"Git Hoffman to the sawbones!" Coulter blustered, in a vain attempt to reassert some authority. "Yuh stayin' around?" he demanded of Hardy. "I aim t' see yuh ag'in, mister. *Yuh've got it comin'!*"

With that he swung surlily on his

72

heel. Kyle recognised the weak threat as the face-saving gesture it was and said nothing. He turned back to the bar and put down a silver dollar alongside his empty glass.

The confrontation was over . . . for now. He heard the batwing doors swinging open and shut on Coulter and Snyder, then again more slowly as Lance Brannigan, Hoffman and the other Triple-Z tough staggered off to lick their wounds.

There was some raucous laughter in the furthest shadows and someone hooted. Whether it was release of nervous tension or plain derision, Kyle couldn't guess.

Kyle took his drink to an empty corner table. Somehow it didn't surprise him when Maria Cortazzi threaded her way sinuously through the thinning crowd to join him.

Red-painted lips curved in a smile. "We show those arrogant *gringo diablos*, no?"

He looked up at her, trying not to

73

let his eyes rove over her lush body as she seated herself across from him.

"Thank you again, ma'am, for talkin' up like you did. I owe you a debt." A thickness had crept into his throat, deepening the tone of his voice.

"It is no big affair, *señor*. Is there not something else I can do for you?" Her eyes met his. They were dark liquid pools of flirtatious promise across the rim of the glass she held to her lips with long, slender fingers. At close quarters, he saw experience was beginning to mar her bloom. Her raven hair was swept back severely from a high forehead and the smoothness of her creamy brow was lightly lined.

He pondered, wondering again how much she could tell him about the altercation that had ended so fatally for Tom Tyler. And he still had the assignment that had brought him here in the first place. "Mebbe you've done enough already. I wouldn't want to make no more trouble for you, ma'am." He glanced across to the bar and the proprietorial Emilio Vicente. "Your boss has got his eye on us."

Her laughter tinkled. "He do not interfere. I have a living to make. I am hostess as well as dancer. It is expected that I should attend at the customers' tables."

Kyle frowned. "It might not look good if you was to talk too much to me. Word might get back to the *hombres* that run this burg, an' they sure ain't got no love for me."

"Then you must come upstairs to my room. There it is private for us to speak and there is love to spare." Her bold eyes left no ambiguity in the invitation.

From the corner of his eye, Kyle had already seen the men at a nearby table nudging one another and cracking lewd jokes in between casting looks in Maria's direction.

Maybe it wasn't such a bad idea. The time and privacy was needed if he was to ask the kind of questions he wanted, and no one among the dirty-minded cow prodders here would suspect their departure upstairs was for anything other than the age-old reasons.

"I often entertain patrons alone, *señor* . . . " she coaxed seductively.

"All right," he agreed levelly. "Lead on, ma'am."

Several stifled sniggers reached his ears when Maria weaved her way through the tables to the narrow stairs at the back of the *cantina*, hips swaying, Kyle in tow.

They didn't see the big stranger sigh, then smile to himself. No doubt they thought he'd now been mesmerised by her obvious charms and was about to pay an extra-handsome price in consideration of his deliverance into her yielding arms from those of the law.

★ ★ ★

Lance Brannigan returned to the *Paloma Blanca* not many minutes after Kyle and Maria had vanished upstairs. He brought with him his surviving Triple-Z escort and Deputy Sheriff Izzy Snyder. "I demand the protection of the law," he told Snyder. "And if I don't get it, my old man will hear about it, y'hear?"

"Ain't this kinda provocative?" Snyder asked.

"No jasper can stop me going where I like!" Lance retorted petulantly. The bitterness of his humiliation was eating into him like acid.

But he was secretly glad to see the rock-fisted, fast-drawing stranger had lit a shuck. Then the word filtered to him that Hardy had not quit but was upstairs with Maria Cortazzi. He cast his pale gaze around the smoke-filled room and saw for himself that the luscious dancer and hostess was no longer in attendance.

"Why, the goddamn sneaky whore! She's got the hots for that bastard. That's why she stuck her bill in an' kept him out of jail." He slammed his soft, beringed fist on the bar counter.

"Vicente! C'me'ere, you rat!"

"*Señor*, I have offended?" Emilio Vicente grovelled before the rich range dandy.

Lance swore. "You damn well bet you have. Your greaser bitch Maria has gone too far this time. An' she's gotta be taught a lesson!"

"*Por Dios!* Anytheeng you want, Señor Brannigan!"

"You said it, *amigo*," Lance said mockingly. "I seem to remember you've got a loan on this shack off a land company and my pa just happens to be in the chair. You'd better be a heap mindful of that!"

Vicente wrung his hands and shook his head in great sorrow. "*Si, si . . .*" he whimpered.

Lance turned back to his *compadres*, a slow, evil grin creeping into his bruised face. "We'll slip back to Doc Chester an' pick up a little something for dear Emilio to feed these lovebirds."

Vicente's mouth dropped open.

"*Madre de Dios!* Ees thees poison you weel breeng me?" His swarthy skin had gone sickly pale and he was trembling. "Maria, she ees not a bad girl," he pleaded, "even eef she no like to sleep weeth you and goes weeth thees devil weeth the clever feests and queek gon — "

"Aw, shut up, you snivelling louse! It'll be just something to give 'em a bellyache and make 'em suffer," Lance promised.

The *cantina* proprietor was eager to believe it. But from the vicious gleam in Lance's pale eyes, Snyder and the Triple-Z tough knew he lied.

★ ★ ★

The upstairs room where Maria Cortazzi plied her second, more lucrative but precarious trade was not much more than a former loft, up under the rafters. A small but open window gave ventilation. And it rid the room of that pungent smell — compounded

79

of liquor, tobacco smoke and unwashed humanity — which was the characteristic of low-class saloons in every frontier town and was so strongly present in the *cantina* downstairs.

The room had a *Chumaco* rug on the floor, a dressing-table with a surprisingly large, tilt-adjustable mirror, and an oak wardrobe hard up against an inner wall. But it was dominated by a huge, iron-framed bed with brass-trimmed bedends and scarlet sheets. There were no chairs.

"Make yourself comfortable, *señor*," Maria said in her low, warm voice, and pushed Kyle back gently. The big man's legs came up against the bed, behind his knees, and he had little choice but to sit down heavily. There was a twanging of wire springs and his backside sank into the softness.

"I don't mean to — uh — take anythin' off you, ma'am, 'cept mebbe a little information."

Laughter gurgled in her throat and she released the clasp that held her hair at the nape of her neck so it tumbled loose in a shiny black cascade. It rippled and brushed across his face when she went to sit close beside him. Involuntarily, he shivered.

She did not comprehend his reluctance. "For you, there will be no paying of *dinero*. I will do it as an especial gift."

"But why?"

"Because you have thrashed that oh-so arrogant pig Lance Brannigan. I hate him! Him and his wicked father and all the bad men they bring to run this town."

"What have they done to you?"

Her dark eyes were stormy with a passion only partly sexual. "They give orders — tell me who I must entertain. To save Emilio and my job, I do what they say, except for one thing. I never let that Lance touch me! He is revolting, that one, and not like the real man."

"I must help you get away from here."

"*Gracias, amigo*, but you must not fret. To go is not what I want. This is the life I choose. My body may be for sale, but my mind and heart I keep for myself."

He wondered what cruel history of hardship, privation and sorrow must lay behind her decision. But in the 1870s, and in such places, these were questions you didn't ask. Besides, he had his own concerns which would give rise to enough inquisition.

"Tell me, what did you know of Tom Tyler? They say he challenged the gunslinger Jules Despard on account of you."

Her face became grave. "Ah, it is such a tragedy, no? He still a child, that one — an innocent." She gave an anguished smile. "He adore my dancing. He tell me I am very beautiful. But he, too, becomes the victim of the Brannigans. It is despicable!"

"The Brannigans?"

"*Exactemente, amigo*. They bring the Despard creature here. I know, because it is for their *dinero* he receive my favours. Emilio tell me. And Despard, he boast to me in this room he come to the valley to kill." She shuddered, her voice sinking almost to a whisper. "He do it for *them*, I think. It is deliberate murder."

Before Kyle could question her more, a rap at the door interrupted them.

"Eet sees I, Emilio, *señor, señorita*. I breeng dreenks."

Maria rose with her dancer's inherent grace and unlatched the door. "What is this, Emilio? We have called for no liquor." She glanced back at Kyle, puzzled.

"*Si*, Maria. Eet ees on the house," the Mexican explained from the shadows of the landing, showing white teeth in an obsequious smile. "There has been mucha bad beesiness. We must make *full* amends to our guest." He grinned suggestively as he thrust a tray with a dusty, foreign-looking bottle and two tall, thin-stemmed glasses on it into Maria's hands. Then he slinked away quickly like a nervous cat.

Kyle watched the woman place the tray amongst the hair brushes and cosmetic pots on the dressing-table. "That won't make this place any better to live in," he growled.

"Come, we must not be churlish. It is surely better than nothing. Maybe Emilio feel guilty." She splashed sparkling white wine into the delicate glasses and examined the faded label. "It is very special this, three Double Eagles a bottle. From across the ocean."

But Kyle, unimpressed, was rummaging in his pants pocket. "Never mind all that foofaraw." He took out a Bull Durham sack. But he wasn't going to build a smoke. Instead of tobacco flakes, the sack contained just one black cheroot butt, wrapped carefully in wheatstraw cigarette papers.

"Maria, I want to show *you* something expensive and unusual. I guess you see all kinds of smokes from quirlies to cigars, but do you know a man hereabouts who uses a brand like this?"

Sipping from a filled glass, Maria leaned over to examine the black stub, the low neck of her white blouse gaping distractingly.

"Why, *si, señor*. There is but one man who smokes these all the time . . . " She stopped haltingly.

"Who is he, Maria?" Kyle pressed urgently.

But Maria didn't answer and the sweet-smelling wine in her glass was suddenly slopping on to his shirt.

"What — ?"

Kyle looked up to see that her eyes were glazed and rolling. All at once the glass slipped from her nerveless fingers and she was falling across him in a senseless heap.

Swiftly, he extricated himself from the luxuriant tresses of her long black hair, and getting up lifted her legs on to the bed.

"God almighty! Maria! Maria!" He gently tapped her face, but she was deeply unconscious, her breathing fast and shallow.

"The drink . . . " he muttered and moved to the dressing-table. When he was surprised by a sudden movement from behind — from the side of the room away from the door — it was already too late.

The hard butt of a solid Frontier Colt smashed down viciously on his skull and he crashed to the floor rug with a solid thump.

6

Sadist's Vengeance

THE trio that entered Maria's room through the doors of the massive oak wardrobe comprised Lance Brannigan, the remaining Triple-Z hard-case sent by his father to watch over him in town, and Izzy Snyder.

The crooked deputy sheriff had crept in first and it was he who had wielded the Colt butt with such devastating effect.

"You better not have cracked his goddamn' head," Lance griped. "My plan depends on the bastard staying alive long enough to suffer for his hell-raising."

Snyder knew Kyle Hardy's immediate death would jeopardise the Sweetwater scheme of things only insofar as Lance would be cheated of the full niceties of his depraved vengeance over the big saddle bum and the tarnished lady who despised him. But he was shrewd enough to play along, seeing potential profit for himself.

"Aw, it was jest a tap. Yuh saw for yuhself he weren't drinkin' none o' yore spiked liquor. An' who told yuh about this sneak entrance from the next room? Saloon whores sometimes need rescuin' from troublesome customers. Good thing this dump was set up with that in mind. An' good thing I knew about it!"

Lance pouted. "Sure, Izzy. But we need Hardy alive for now, to take the blame for what's going to happen to this bitch. Judas! She's going to pay for her insults and loose-tongued interfering! Just leave her to me." His pale eyes were fever-bright.

"Yeah, it stuck in my craw to see the way she made a monkey outa ol' Coulter." The lanky deputy spat in the palms of his hands and rubbed them together. "Let's get on with it, pard," he told the third man. "We gotta lug this ranny down the back stairs to the yard. Lance can get right on an' fix things here how he wants."

Lance grinningly seized the thirty-dollar bottle of European wine and tipped the rest of its contents over Kyle Hardy's head, but the unconscious man scarcely groaned as the other pair dragged him out.

Left alone with the drugged woman, Lance could not control the trembling excitement that flushed his sallow features. The pleasure of a sadistic triumph was his for the taking.

"*Puta!*" he spat gloatingly, sending spittle to fleck Maria Cortazzi's strewn black hair. "Now I have you where I want you." No one bucked a Brannigan. For that, she was going to pay in full before she died.

As he violated her supine body, he reflected it was a great pity she could only lie so heavy and so still.

★ ★ ★

By the light of the three-quarter moon Jules Despard, sitting tall in the saddle of a raw-boned and streaky dun that matched him for size, wended his way through Sweetwater Valley. Behind him followed a pack horse bred on more normal lines, standing several hands shorter, its lead rein attached to the cantle of Despard's saddle. About him rode an aura of total malevolence.

Despard's hawkish face was all hard planes and angles in the stark moonglow. As ever, his eyes were two colourless mirrors emotion didn't touch. Yet had there been others to witness his passing along the lonesome trail, it would have been sensed that Despard was wound up with deep and venomous anger, like a snake readied to strike.

A coyote in the silver mountains beyond howled dismally. The valley had become the Valley of Death.

At a fork in the trail on the crest of a rise was a plank neatly inscribed with a hot iron and attached to an

90

oak sapling. It pointed Despard to the Triple-Z outfit. The black-garbed gunfighter grunted his satisfaction, for this was his destination.

It was just a few more minutes' journey to the arched trailside entrance to the sprawling ranch. On the rolling grasslands that stretched behind, Despard saw the dark shapes of longhorns bedded down for the night. He rode in, down a tree-lined path. It was fully another fifteen minutes before he rounded a bend and came upon the ranch buildings of the Triple-Z, at the foot of a low hill.

The ranch-house itself was big and handsome, built in stone, *hacienda* style, and porticoed. Set away from it, across a gravel yard, was a cluster of other buildings, lumber-built, and including a long, narrow bunkhouse. The other structures, Despard guessed, were stables and storehouses and a smithy. A string of sleek ponies was rounded up in a corral beneath the overhang of a huge mariposa tree.

He smelled big money.

Despard dismounted by an oak halfway down the hillside. He took out his two worn-gripped Colts and span the chambers to check each iron was fully loaded. Then he straightened his flat-crowned black Stetson and leaving the horses ground-tied strode out purposefully for the ranch-house.

Dogs barked and snapped on long rope leashes as the gaunt intruder stalked into the yard.

A ranch-hand toting an unaimed carbine rushed out of the bunkhouse, peering into the gloom. "Hold it right there, mister, an' state your business!"

The shaft of light spilling from the open doorway of the lamplit bunkhouse etched his outline for Despard clearly. But the Triple-Z man saw only a lean-shanked shadowy figure before crimson gun flame stabbed from out of the darkness and the carbine was wrenched from his grasp by the slam of a .45 bullet.

"Button your lip an' quiet them

hounds afore I fill 'em with holes," Despard rasped.

Other hands appeared in the bunkhouse doorway. But Despard had sprung like a cougar into the centre of the moonlit yard. The sight of the menacing gunslinger with a smoking Colt in his bony fist deterred rash moves.

The shaken man who'd challenged Despard made no attempt to retrieve his shattered carbine, but moved over to muzzle the frantic dogs.

The ruckus could scarcely escape notice in the big house. A man appeared at the porticoed door. "What in hell's name is going on out there?" he yelled down from the top of the steps.

"Are you Bart Brannigan?" Despard croaked back. His voice was like the harsh cry of a buzzard denied its feast.

"What's it to you if I am, mister?" He spoke with the self-importance of a man unused to questioning.

"'Cause if'n you are, you an' me got

fat to chew. The name's Despard."

Brannigan sneered. "The gun-slick, huh? What call would you have to come busting in here?"

"It's on account o' your son. A *private* matter, Brannigan."

A faint glimmer of what might have been concern flitted across the cattle baron's fleshy face. Maybe if his son was involved he could not choose to be so indifferent.

He swallowed some of his considerable pride. "All right boys. I can handle this. Put up your gun, Despard, and step inside."

Brannigan was a burly, well-fed man in his fifties, sleekly groomed and attired in a three-piece broadcloth suit with a heavy gold watch-chain across his broad chest. His wealthy appearance was at one with the richness of the lavishly furnished room into which he led the gunfighter, who instantly looked out of place in well-worn black clothes dusty from the trail.

No less than eight hanging lamps

illuminated the formal room with its carved cedarwood table, chairs and dresser. Fancy ornaments and willow-patterned chinaware decorated the shelves of the dresser and the heels of Despard's boots sank into the carpet. Thick red drapes were drawn across the windows and were too new to show any sign of fading from the sun.

But Despard was not the kind to be intimidated. The display merely deepened his cold anger and resolve.

Brannigan sloshed whiskey from a heavy cut-glass decanter into a fist-sized glass. Rudely and deliberately, he offered none to his visitor, but tossed the liquor down in a single gulp.

"Let's hear you then, Despard," he demanded. "What's this with my son?"

"Plumb curious thing how the rich can shy off payin' their bills," Despard grated.

The slug of fiery whiskey hit Brannigan's stomach. The uneasiness he'd felt when this gun-toter had first mentioned his son was cauterised. His habitual confidence seeped back. He was fortified. Hell, he was Big Bart Brannigan, boss of the valley. This Despard might be one of the fastest guns around, but he was an underling just the same — a man for hire when there was a need for his talents.

He considered Despard's oblique reply. "You got some complaint, feller?" he asked contemptuously.

"You hear about events in town?"

"A thing or two." Brannigan put light to a black cheroot with a lucifer.

Despard nodded, his bleak eyes slitted. "I reckon. Regular fire-eater, eh, that boy o' your'n? But he didn't have enough sand to face down Tyler, who was just a green kid. I figure you know'd he got me to do that?"

Brannigan stuck the cheroot between his curling lips and hooked his thumbs in the armholes of his vest. "Your — uh — business arrangements are no concern of mine," he said distastefully.

Despard droned on in the same passionless but chilling monotone.

"Kinda loco streak your son has, Brannigan. Shortchanges me. Tells me he'll see me in hell afore he hands over the rest of the bounty he'd agreed to payin'."

Brannigan, who shared all his son's high-handed arrogance, considered the sentiment a worthy one. But he carefully put down his cheroot. "Have you come here to ask *me* to meet this alleged debt?" he asked incredulously.

"I ain't come to take the night air."

Brannigan shook his head, clutched his right forearm with his left hand and turned as though to refill the empty whiskey glass on the sideboard. But the move was a feint. His left hand had pressed a spring clip inside his sleeve, releasing a sneak derringer concealed there. The stubby-barrelled gun slipped down into his right palm and when he turned back he had it pointed.

"Hoist 'em, gun-slick, or I'll shoot you down like the vermin you are!"

The fastest gun in Arizona couldn't beat a man who had already drawn.

Despard regarded him with icy scorn, but didn't waste breath on any reply. Not yet. He merely raised his hands.

"Clem! Walt!" Brannigan bawled. Jerky with excitement he closed in on Despard till he was not much more than an arm's reach away. At this range, a .44 calibre slug would blast a hole clear through the gunhawk, and he felt very safe.

The two hardbitten henchmen he'd summoned burst into the room, six-shooters drawn, ready for trouble.

"Get this mangy bum outa here!" he ordered. "Put him on his cayuse an' see to it he hightails it off the Triple-Z."

Clem's thumb was on the hammer of his Colt. It snapped back with a loud and ominous click. Walt gestured Despard toward the door with his levelled weapon and Brannigan put up his derringer.

Only then did Despard speak, the words harsh like a file on steel. "You got the drop on me but you're makin' a bad mistake this evenin', Brannigan.

98

A miscalculation. Word's gonna get around, to the law mebbe — "

"Word!" Brannigan jeered, made bold by his rout of the gunman. "Who'll take the word of a jasper with your reputation against that of a respectable citizen?"

He drew on his cheroot and puffed blue smoke into Despard's face, playing to the gallery of his crew. "Besides, I got the Sweetwater law right here," he said, slapping his pocket. "Vamoose, mister!"

"Walk!" growled Clem, gesturing threateningly with his Colt. And the notorious Jules Despard was bundled out.

7

Prisoner

KYLE HARDY was caught in a monstrous pounding of hoofs. He knew he was lying prone someplace in the dark. He'd been thrown and was in the dust. A stampede! He'd be trampled to death by a thousand cows . . . storm-spooked, rampaging, lumbering over him, black eyes bulging, horns tossing.

He started to struggle to his feet, wondering where he might be. The pounding became a roaring in his head. Nausea gripped his belly. It was only then he became aware he wasn't trapped in some prairie bedlam; that it was all inside his own head.

Groaning — forcing himself to take deep, steadying breaths — he raised a hand and felt the stickiness of blood at the back of his scalp. And remembered. He'd been bushwhacked. Gunclubbed in the room of Maria the *cantina* hostess after she'd been taken mysteriously ill.

"No, doped," he muttered, the suspicion hardening into certainty.

He staggered to a flight of wooden stairs he could make out rising steeply up the back of a building and sat on the lowest step. All his clothes now reeked of the same sweet wine he recalled Maria spilling on his shirt. He could hear the buzz of a social crowd. Interspersing it was the occasional burst of revelry and the tinkling of a piano and the strumming of a guitar. He figured he was in an enclosed yard at the back of the *Paloma Blanca*.

He heard urgent footfalls again and knew that this time they were real and human. He lurched to his feet and the roaring started again inside his head, blurring his vision.

A group of men was suddenly bursting into the yard, bringing the yellow illumination of a bobbing lantern that sent grotesque shadows leaping up the wall of the *cantina*.

Izzy Snyder's nasal voice said harshly. "There he is, pardners. What a stroke o' luck. Looks like the crazy bastard's taken a tumble down the back stairs."

Sheriff Lief Coulter pushed his ample belly to the front of the party and shoved his drawn Colt under Kyle's nose.

"I'm takin yuh in, yuh sonofabitch! I shoulda done it right off. Yuh looked like yuh *was* on the dodge, even if there weren't no 'wanted' poster. Put the cuffs on 'im, Deputy!"

"Hey, what the hell is this?" Kyle protested.

"Jesus, hear 'im play the innocent!" Snyder snarled through his straggly whiskers.

"I suppose yuh got good reason to be skulking in this yard?" Coulter said with heavy sarcasm.

"Sure," Kyle shot back, the adamant word sending his head spinning afresh. "I was hit over the head and dumped here. I got the bump and the blood to prove it."

"The lyin' toad!" Snyder accused. "He cracked his noggin fallin' down them stairs. It's plain as the nose on my face!"

"Ain't no woman to sugar-talk yuh outa this one," the sheriff said. The hissing lantern made bright pinpricks in his piggy eyes. He shook his head disgustedly. "Yuh made sure o' that when yuh raped and murdered her, though it beats all hell why."

★ ★ ★

If Jules Despard had a god it was money. He was a man without feeling, plying a grisly trade in sudden death. Certainly he didn't know the meaning of the word mercy. Nor, as the cold professional, were anger and hatred conceded a place in the normal run of his life.

But he rode away from the Triple-Z home-lot on his plodding dun with a

103

hot rage smouldering in his brain. He'd been duped, cheated, mocked. What kind of sucker did these Brannigans think he was that they believed he could let them hoodwink him? Of necessity, the score would have to be settled. His most precious commercial asset, his reputation, was at stake.

Men could fear him or despise him as they chose. But they could not cross him.

And Bart Brannigan had had the gall to draw a sneak gun on him. Despard knew his points of law well. In his trade a man needed to. It was an offence to carry a concealed weapon. If you toted a gun it had to be worn in plain sight. But like Brannigan had said, he *was* the law in this valley.

Despard paid no mind to a rising wind off the mountains that swirled the trail dust and brought a nip to the air. Not even to turn up the collar of his black coat. Maybe he was insensible to such minor irritations. But it wasn't that his senses weren't finely tuned. To certain things they were, for ever. That was the way of him and possibly the secret of his survival in the untamed territories he roamed.

Consequently, he heard the approaching rider many vital seconds before another might. His predator's ears picked up the rapid clop of a horse at full gallop borne on the wind. He *felt* the sound of the hoofs thrumming through the hard-baked dirt of the trail he rode.

He assessed his situation in a raking glance. A short distance off the scrub-fringed trail was a shadowy clump of knotty pine. Without hesitation he dug his booted heels into the flanks of the dun, jerked up its drooping head, and veered his horses off the trail. Loose stones that had been kicked out to the perimeter of the trail by regular use were scattered in his purposeful haste.

Reaching the trees, Despard reined in and waited, confident that though the cover was sparse the approaching rider wouldn't see him or his two beasts in the darkness. Any moment now the rider should be looming into view across the undulating terrain.

Despard recognised him instantly. He uttered a growling curse. It was the two-timing dude Lance Brannigan, leaning forward intently over his showy palomino's neck, kicking hard with his silver-spurred heels.

That gold-coated palomino, with its flowing snow-white mane and tail, was like a goad to Despard. Such animals were uncommon, bred from special lines, and worth many thousands of dollars. To the Brannigan boy it was just another plaything: to treat, even to ruin, as he saw fit. Its flanks glistened with a lather of sweat. The smell of hot horseflesh reached Despard on an eddy of the night wind. Despard was unbothered by the horse's treatment, but the selfish wealth it represented was a galling prod to his own injury.

Cheated of his *dinero* — his life's blood — by an arrogant young spendthrift . . .

The magnificent animal scented the

106

nearness of other horses and gave a shrill whinny when it passed the spot where Despard had left the trail. But the Brannigan kid just gave some curt, unintelligible cry and yanked at the reins, setting the palomino's straying nose down the trail.

It threw up its head with a jingling of bit-pieces in square yellow teeth and eyes rolling wildly, white mane flowing, plunged on.

The kid was plainly in the grip of a great excitement, Despard figured sourly. He grinned without mirth. Riding at such a suicidal pace, maybe he would break his neck. But then maybe not. In fact, he didn't hold out much hope of it happening. Both horse and rider knew the trail too well for sure, and the moon was riding high in a star-flecked cloudless sky.

Despard thought some more. Until the Brannigans' debt was paid, their business was his business. By nature, he wasn't the snooping kind, but it could do no harm to try and learn what this big rush was all about. Could be he might turn it to his own advantage . . .

Whatever, it took a hell of a lot more than a scummy crew of cow-waddies to scare him away, and these goddamned range bosses were going to get their needings sometime.

He ripped out an oath, picked his way back to the trail and set off at a canter through the still settling dust that marked the hell-for-leather ride of the scion of the Triple-Z.

★ ★ ★

Big Bart Brannigan refilled the big glass tumbler and tossed down its fiery contents. It was the third slug of rye he'd swallowed since the departure of his uninvited visitor.

It was in the nature of the man that he wouldn't admit, even to himself, that Jules Despard had rattled him. But it was an incontrovertible fact that he was seeking something, be it courage or consolation, and that his session of hard drinking had begun in the presence of the dangerous, harsh-voiced gunhawk.

He was nagged, too, by the absence of his son. He tugged out his heavy gold watch and scowled at it, eyes burning beneath his heavy brows. Young Lance could do no wrong, of course, but maybe he shouldn't have dragged this Despard into their affairs. Despard was a man to be afraid of, if you admitted you could be afraid.

Then again, it had disposed of Old John Tyler's uppity boy real neatly. Too bad this saddle-bum — what was his name? — Hardy, had horned in. Without his son, Tyler would have been so short-handed he could have been knuckling under in no time. With just his girl, sassy though she might be, and two deadbeats for hands, the cripple Tyler hadn't a show of running the Diamond-T. Now that didn't seem so certain.

But Lance had gone back to town to sort that one out, hadn't he? Every man had his price, and that would go for this Hardy for sure. These drifters didn't amount to much when it came to regular hard work. He'd take the better offer, hang around awhile, then mosey off.

With their new hand whipped away from them, the Tylers would see sense . . . he might even force them to settle for a *lower* price. The thought pleased Brannigan and he chuckled coldly. His shaking hand chinked his empty glass against others as he set it down on the sideboard.

Soon, the whole valley would be his, end to end, mountain to mountain. The vision he'd nursed all these years, since the death of his dear Elena and the birth of his wonderful Lance, would come true. All the little men would be gone. The stupid ones. The weak ones. Bit by bit he'd gobbled up their small spreads. Those who had dared to oppose him, he'd trampled into the dust. You bought them, beat them or killed them.

He was lighting another cheroot when he heard a single horse clatter into the yard and the cocky shout of his son's voice.

"Hey! Unsaddle and rub down my horse, will ya!"

His son alone . . . Bart Brannigan was immediately anxious to know what had happened to the two men who'd ridden out with him, a pair of specially picked hands he'd not hired for their skills in tending cattle.

"Where's Hoffman and Vaughn?" he demanded as Lance burst into the big ranch-house, his face flushed and sweaty with excitement.

The younger Brannigan scowled. "Aw, don't worry 'bout them. They'll be following. Hoffman ran into trouble."

"Trouble?"

The anxious father noted for the first time the swellings and splits on his boy's face. Had Lance been in a fist fight?

"Don't worry, I said. It's taken care of — and some! Jest wait till you hears this!"

Bart Brannigan's head was buzzing with questions and the generous consumption of whiskey. "What went wrong?" he demanded, irritable at being in the dark.

He'd already had the bad experience of having to handle Despard when he'd come calling, mouthing off his insolent insults. Somehow he still hadn't gotten around in his warped mind to finding any fault with Lance for that. Now the young man himself had showed. And his wild aspect and story gave cause only for parental concern of the most selfish kind. Was Lance himself in trouble? What would it cost him to get him out of it?

"Hardy played up some an' made free with his fists and shooter," Lance told him. "But he's fixed. An' so's that Cortazzi bitch who spoke up for him. She'd been asking for hers for a long time."

He licked his lips lasciviously and his pale eyes glistened in the brightness of the many hanging lamps. His mind was dwelling for the hundredth time on the gratifing and thorough manner in which he'd salved his wounded pride.

"I gave it to her, Pa, mighty good. It's all even-steven. She's dead . . . an' best of all, that Hardy is gonna swing at the end of a rope for it!"

Listening intently, Brannigan senior settled down in a big horsehair armchair and puffed blue smoke toward the ceiling in a stream while Lance began to fill him in on some of the details. His confidence started to seep back.

The boy had returned safe and as the minutes wore on that was making him feel a lot better. It sounded, too, like he'd been pushing things in the right direction. He had brains, did young Lance; he was a son a man could be proud of. Quick-thinking. Ruthless.

The interfering saddle-bum sounded as good as dead; throwing a murder charge at him was a smart idea, so much better than smashing his head to a pulp and killing him outright but creating a mystery and maybe a martyr. He barked a coarse, brutal laugh.

"Nothing left unexplained, eh? Never a good thing to leave loose ends for nosy dogs to worry at. That Cortazzi whore was getting ideas above her station, it sounds like. So she's no loss either."

He rubbed his beefy hands together with satisfaction, remembering how he himself had given Jules Despard his marching orders also. Things were working out just fine for the Brannigan clan.

Lance postscripted his vile narrative with a determined plea.

"An' it's time we had a word with the Law and Order Committee, Pa. Coulter ain't got enough guts. It's time we had Snyder for sheriff," he finished.

Bart nodded. "It'll be done, Son, you can damn' well bet on it. Next elections, or sooner."

There were twelve people on the committee; he himself was chairman. Six of the others were his tools, so he was always sure of the casting vote. It wouldn't be hard to get shot of Coulter.

Now his devious mind was clearing and racing ahead. Other uses were to be made of this very satisfactory situation surely? Something, he knew, was struggling to present itself through the whiskey fumes and pungent smoke.

Suddenly, the inspired thought rushed upon him. He got the picture, complete, wicked and bloody.

"The Tylers!" he snapped. "Now's the time we get rid of this whole goddamn business in one swoop, Son. You've set it up doggone handy for us. Get the boys together. Have 'em saddle you a fresh bronc."

Lance stared, pouting. "For what, Pa?"

"We're riding out to the Diamond-T tonight. It's time to hit 'em. I've had a gutful of this circling around Old John

Tyler, with him sorta hissing back like a rattler on the prod."

"Yeah, it sticks in the craw right enough."

"Waal, before daybreak it's all gonna be sewed up. There's nothing can stop us. Listen . . . "

★ ★ ★

Outside the Brannigan *hacienda*, a dark figure slipped across the yard and melted into the inky-black shadow at the side of the house. He had a gun drawn from one of his twin holsters and his finger was round the trigger, his thumb on the hammer.

No dogs barked. Still muzzled, Despard concluded with an exultant grin. So that gamble had paid off. He cat-footed along the wall to where a splinter of light marked the thickly-curtained window of the room where an hour earlier he'd bandied words with Bart Brannigan.

Sure enough, Brannigan junior

was speaking with his father. The windows were ajar and Despard listened attentively. It was no strain on his ears.

Above the omnipresent hum of night insects Lance's voice carried to him shrill and clear. It was full of ghoulish glee and smug self-congratulation. His father's tones had the same cruel edge, but his speech was deeper and harder; his words more considered.

Despard heard as much of their shenanigans as he needed to hear. Then, his face wolfish bleak, he glided away again into the darkness.

8

Secret Weapon

THE jail block was at the back of the Sweetwater Springs courthouse, reached through Sheriff Coulter's office by way of a passage and a stout door. The cells were facing this door, three in a row, with heavy grille doors across the fronts. Ventilation for each cell was provided by a high, small, barred window set into the thick adobe wall at the rear. All of the cells were unoccupied.

Relieved of his gun belt, Kyle Hardy was unceremoniously bundled into the centre cell. It had one narrow, hard-looking, built-in bunk. Stencilled markings on a single tatty grey blanket proclaimed it the one-time property of the US Cavalry. In a corner was an insanitary pail full of foul-smelling slops.

"Welcome to the calaboose, mister!" said Coulter. "The circuit judge sits in two days' time, so yuh got plenty o' time to repent your sins afore yuh goes to the gallows."

The heavy grille door swung shut on Hardy and the sheriff locked it with a large key carried on a jangling bunch.

"You're makin' a helluva mistake, Sheriff," Kyle protested. "I wouldn't have killed Maria Cortazzi. Why should I? An' that means you're lettin' the real killer walk loose out there! One day it's not gonna look so good on your record."

Coulter flushed. "None o' your lip. We got yuh red-handed, yuh dirty coyote!"

Snyder laughed hollowly. "He won't give in, Sheriff, will he? Maybe we should rough him up a bit. Rape and murder don't deserve no less."

Coulter harrumphed officiously. "That's as mebbe, Deputy. Howsumever, much as I 'preciate your personal hankerin' for justice, we'll do it all legal-like. Go out an' find Seth Hetrick, then yuh can go off duty. The ol'-timer can sit in as night jailer."

Snyder shrugged heavily. He put down the lantern he was still carrying, which was the only illumination in the cell block. "Sure thing, Sheriff," he acceded and shuffled off.

In fact, the arrangement suited Snyder fine, for he had irons of his own in the fire and now was the time to tend them.

Kyle realised he was in a desperate situation. His life hung in the balance. It seemed highly unlikely he would be given a fair trial in this corrupt town. He didn't even have a lawyer to defend him. Any who practised in the territory, he suspected, would be under the thumb of Brannigan or others of his cattlemen's syndicate crowd.

When Snyder had gone he made another attempt to sway Lief Coulter. "You should do some more investigatin', Sheriff. Someone's tryin' to pull the wool over your eyes. I'm innocent, I tell you. Maria had *helped* me. You know that. I had no cause to kill her."

But the boneheaded sheriff wasn't to be budged. As far as he was concerned he had the killer behind bars and he had no intention of digging into the affairs of a saloon whore who, rumour would have it, had on occasion numbered several prominent citizens among her clientele.

No, this solution suited him just fine. There would be votes to lose at the next elections by taking any other course. Most importantly, the Brannigans would be happy to watch this jasper Hardy swing, and that could do him no harm at all.

"The case agin yuh is watertight, Hardy," he said conclusively. "Yuh went up to her room with her. I got dozens of witnesses. And yuh was found senseless at the bottom of the stairs back of her place. Hell, what more does it need?"

"A motive mebbe?"

"I reckon yuh was loco drunk when yuh did it an' don't remember."

"But she was drugged an' I was gun-clubbed."

"Aw, shut up, will ya! We don't wanna go through that agin. Your story's full o' holes an' short on corroboration."

Coulter was sticking irascibly and adamantly to the theory he thought best suited his own interests, even if it didn't hold up in every particular.

"You're making a blunder, Coulter. And one day soon Sweetwater Valley's gonna see how big a blunder," Kyle bluffed.

"Shut up, I tell yuh! Yuh talkin' a lotta hot air."

Kyle thought of the Diamond-T and wondered what interpretation would be put on his failure to return. Specifically, the picture kept coming to his mind of an attractive, fair-haired girl with cornflower blue eyes serious and sad in a sun-bronzed face.

He didn't like the idea that Verity Tyler might think he'd changed his mind and behaved like the rootless drifter he so obviously looked. Wandering cowpokes rambled all over the West, from North Dakota to Texas and Missouri to Nevada. They took jobs when the urge took them, generally when they were stony broke, and pushed on again just as casually.

Would Verity think he was one of the feckless kind; that he'd decided to renege on his promise and leave the Diamond-T in the lurch?

To think that she might believe he'd broken his word made him feel bitter to an unwarranted degree.

"Sheriff," he called. "Can you grant me one favour? There's a message I want sendin' to the folks I signed on with at the Diamond-T."

Coulter laughed his harsh scorn. "Favours! Hell, big boy, we don't give no favours to perverts and killers hereabouts," he sneered.

Kyle moved away from the bars

and slumped down wearily on the bunk. Goddamnit, if it wasn't that two people had died violently in the past twelve hours and his own neck was now at risk, the whole business would be farcically funny.

But those were the dire circumstances, and it gave him cold shudders and an empty, nervous feeling in the pit of his stomach knowing he was in the tightest corner of his life. They were trying to pin Maria's murder on him. Someone was making a bald-faced attempt to railroad him to a hangnoose, and the sheriff was going right along with it.

* * *

Sweetwater Springs was abuzz with excitement despite the lateness of the hour. Both the Scarlet Crescent and the *Paloma Blanca* were doing a roaring trade. News of the ravishing and murder of Maria Cortazzi had spread like wildfire. Liquor was mopped up with the shocking details of the crime.

Then replenishments slaked the throats that got dry with the avid telling and the more lurid retelling.

Even Emilio Vicente himself got more than a little drunk. Which was maybe little wonder, because the proprietor of the *cantina* was shrewd enough to know that the day Maria Cortazzi had walked across his stoop with her battered tin trunk was the luckiest in his life. Her talents had been quickly lauded around the valley and the impression she'd made had shown on Vicente's profit sheet these past two years, too.

Now the goose that laid the golden eggs was dead.

"*Dios mio!*" he groaned. "Eet ees a calameety. Maria keelled! I theenk I weell be seeck when I seen her body."

Izzy Snyder lolled across the bar and patted his brown hand. "But if it's any consolation we got the bastard who did it, Emilio."

"Eet ees so hard to believe. Theese

125

same man, he upset the yo'ng Meester Brannigan. But Maria, she like. Eet sees Meester Brannigan I theenked weell harm her, weeth hees special dreenk to make their bellies ache — "

"Hey, yuh'd better forgit that ever happened, Emilio," Snyder advised. He winked and lowered his voice. "Yuh wouldn't want to get dragged into this trouble yourself now, would you?"

Vicente paled. "But eet was just the leetle joke, *señor!*"

"Sure it was. Now the sooner this skunk Hardy's hanged an' the whole business blows over, the better, huh?"

"But thees beeg stranger, he maybe weell tell the jodge I breeng the dreenk." Vicente was all frowning alarm.

Snyder drew back, looked owlish and pulled a glum mouth beneath his straggly moustache. "Hmm . . . yuh could be right at that. A risky business." His face was not reassuring.

Vicente blinked and trembled. "Reesk, *señor?* For me?"

126

The deputy dug into his pocket, shaking his head mournfully. He slapped a fistful of coins on the bar top. "Break out another bottle of that *vino* yuh's drinkin', Emilio. Hell of a thing findin' Maria like that. An' now this ratbag saddle-bum'll do his best to implicate yuh for sairtain."

"But I am eenocent!"

"Why, o' course yuh are. I know yuh wouldn't harm a fly, Emilio. Course, the best thing would be if'n there weren't no trial."

"No trial?"

"Waal, it'd be best all round, don't yuh reckon? We know it was this here saddle-bum that went loco an' did it. Weren't no *drink* that dealt to Maria . . . so why do we need awkward questions? Listen to the boys, will yuh? They's real mad about what the big bastard did."

Vicente mustered his half-drunken indignation. "And so am I, *Señor* Snyder!"

"Yuh know what I think? Personally,

o' course, seein's how I gotta tote a badge of office an' can't put it around mesself." Snyder preened his whiskers and tried to adopt an air of hamstrung responsibility.

"What ees eet, *señor*?"

Snyder leaned forward to make his suggestion seem all the more confidential. "I figger this was as cold-blooded a murder as we'll ever see, an' Hardy's as guilty as all hell. We shouldn't be waitin' for the law to get around to fixin' up a necktie party for the big galoot. We should encourage the boys to string 'im up tonight!"

Vicente, eyes bulging, fought a battle with himself. Finally he said defiantly, "*Si, amigo*, we owe it to Maria."

"That's right, Emilio ol' pard. And it's so much surer an' *safer*. Eliminates them kinda risky questions we was talkin' about."

Snyder smiled slyly into his glass, swallowed more rye, and congratulated himself on how well his plan was working out. It would only take

Maria's desolated ex-boss to start the lynch talk and the well-oiled, simmering cowhands packing the smoky room would take it up.

He could see them storming the calaboose now, dragging Hardy out to his death. And what would Coulter do? Either way, it didn't matter.

If the sheriff tried to resist in his flabby way, he would be swept aside. If he went along, he would be open to later condemnation for failure to fulfil his proper duty as a lawman.

Both courses would suit Snyder's book. He knew he could count on Lance Brannigan's support when Coulter was tossed out on grounds of incompetence. New elections for sheriff, with himself as victor, would be inevitable.

★ ★ ★

Kyle Hardy sat on the hard bunk in his cell and clutched his aching head in his hands. Sheriff Coulter had long left the smelly jailhouse for the comforts of his office and his place was taken by Seth Hetrick, an old man with a bushy grey beard and bow legs. And a shotgun.

Hetrick seemed to put a lot of pride and faith into this piece of hardware, as well he might. Any sign of trouble and the ten-gauge could blow a hole through a man. Nor did it need gunfighter skills to do it.

The wizened old jasper seemed slightly deaf and Kyle didn't bother to try holding conversation with him, knowing anyway that it would be pointless.

Soon, nursing his shotgun, Hetrick dozed off.

Kyle's thoughts returned once more to the Diamond-T and the Tylers. They were really the only people he'd properly met in this community; the only ones he could even hope might try to help him. But would they have the chance, time, or inclination to do so?

He liked to kid himself the girl would. It would depend largely on how the news reached her, no doubt. Probably some loudmouth would impart the news to the foreman Hammond or the ranch-hand Ellison with plenty of gory detail. Would Verity really believe he'd gone off his head and raped and killed Maria Cortazzi?

He'd have no allies among the hardbitten crews that rode for Brannigan and his stooges. And the townsfolk would be too scared to lift a hand, even if he could convince anyone at his coming trial that were they witnessing a travesty of justice.

The judge, he had a sneaking fear, would be virtually Bart Brannigan's guest while in town; he couldn't hope that the rancher would have overlooked the court in his thorough arrangements to rule the Sweetwater Valley roost.

Kyle was jerked out of his grim reverie by a pattering noise from the next cell. He knew he was the only prisoner in the three-cell block. Rats?

Across the stomped earth floor outside, beside the single lantern, Hetrick snored and shifted in his sleep. The chair creaked to his sway but he didn't wake.

Suddenly, a shower of sand and small stones descended on Kyle's head with the same pattering noise he'd heard before.

What the hell is this, he asked himself. He got up on the bunk and cautiously peered out the barred window. Someone was throwing dirt into the cells. But why?

Across the alley, lit only by the stars, he thought he glimpsed a deeper pool of blackness crouched in the darkness of a doorway opposite. The form of a man in a flat-crowned hat was just faintly discernible. He ducked down again quickly. You could trust no one in this godforsaken town and he didn't want to become the target for an assassin's bullet.

The dirt, he surmised, may very well have been thrown to ascertain which of the three cells was occupied. He couldn't think of any other explanation than some strange lunacy.

He'd only just reseated himself on the bunk, pondering the motives of the dirt thrower, when something heavy and hard tumbled through the bars above his head. It landed on the grubby grey blanket beside him with a whoosh and a thump.

Seth Hetrick awoke with a snort. He leaped to his feet, upsetting the loose-jointed chair. The shotgun clattered to the ground.

Kyle caught his breath, for a second dreading the lethal thing would go off, exploding its belly-ripping load in God knew what direction. Almost as a reflex he flipped the loose end of the blanket over the fallen object.

"What in damnation are yuh doin' of, yuh mad dog?"

"Nothin', old-timer."

"Horse-shit! Yuh hit somethin'. I heerd yuh!"

"Just my head against the wall mebbe."

The oldster limped up to the bars, pointing the scattergun ahead of him, cussing under his breath. Kyle stood up and edged to a side wall.

"Guess there ain't much to see inside these four walls."

"None o' the smart talk, young feller." Hetrick's rheumy eyes swivelled in their sockets, taking in the spartan confines of the cell. He looked disappointed when they picked out nothing untoward. He lowered the threatening ten-gauge.

Kyle gave him a lopsided grin and shrugged. "A bad dream mebbe," he drawled with easy sympathy.

Seth Hetrick growled and staggered back to where his overturned chair had come to rest, legs up, against the wall. "Ornery crittur . . . " he mumbled into his beard.

He swallowed the cold remains of the coffee in an enamelled mug, spat into one of the empty cells, righted his chair and sat himself down again. Before long, his head was nodding. And not much later he was back to a wheezy, rhythmic snoring.

Kyle uncovered the object that had been thrown in through the high barred window. It was a .45 Colt Civilian Peacemaker. The gun was well-worn, but clean and oiled. Its trigger had been carefully filed off. It was a gunfighter's weapon. He span the cylinder. Each of the six chambers was loaded.

He hefted the big gun thoughtfully and whistled softly. "Well, what d'you know?"

Somewhere, somehow, he had a helping hand in Sweetwater Springs. He tucked the Colt down inside the waistband of his pants. What would happen next, he didn't know, but that heavy hunk of metal alleviated the despair of what had been total vulnerability. With it came a shred of comfort and hope.

Spirits raised, he began some hard thinking along new lines.

9

Battle with a Lynch Mob

THE town was coming to the boil. In various stages of inebriation, men were tumbling out from saloon and *cantina* and other establishments up and down Main Street and its less salubrious tributaries. They had one idea on their minds.

"Lynch 'im!"

"String 'im up!"

Subtly incited by the crooked deputy sheriff Izzy Snyder, Emilio Vicente of the *Paloma Blanca*, bereft promoter of the late Maria Cortazzi of dancing and other fame, had performed exactly as required.

The suggestion had been put about that an impromptu necktie party, with Kyle Hardy as guest of honour,

and his humiliation of Lance Brannigan earlier in the day; they knew their bosses would smile on their efforts. The rest were the weak and easily led; normally cringing townsfolk who'd drowned misgivings with free booze to the point where the stirrings of righteous indignation overcame the twinges of conscience.

The blood lust had taken over from reason.

"There ain't one scrap o' doubt he's guilty as hell," was a commonly muttered reassurance.

"The sooner he's under the ground, the better."

"Yeah, we'll grab 'im outa the calaboose an' dangle 'im from a cottonwood limb!"

Sheriff Lief Coulter, reading a newspaper in his office with his heels plumped on his scarred desktop, got the first hint of trouble when he heard a rumble of many voices raised in ragged concert and a scuff and tramp of boots like an out-of-step army on the march.

"Sure is a lotta activity out there this late hour, an' it ain't even payday," he cogitated.

Within a moment, he realised the sounds were getting mighty close. Some of these late roisterers were turning into the alley that led to his office and jail behind the courthouse.

Tossing aside the news-sheet, he swung his feet to the floor and scrambled up. Dark shapes appeared behind the frosted glass pane in his office door.

"Open up, Sheriff! Open up!"

"What in damnation's goin' on out thar?" Coulter waddled to the door and injudiciously unlocked it.

The minute the catch snicked back, the door was shoved into Coulter's doltish face. He made a grab for his shooting-iron. But he quickly changed his mind when he comprehended he was already staring down the black muzzle of a drawn .45.

"We come fer the prisoner, Lawman," a ringleader said. "No personal malice intended, but majority opinion figgers the murderin' saddle-bum's too dirty to breathe good Sweetwater air any longer."

Coulter jibbered. "Wh-what yuh gonna do?"

"We're gonna stretch his neck!"

"Yuh can't do that!"

"Jest watch us, Sheriff."

Another Brannigan rannie added with a leer, "Stand in our way an' yuh's liable to wind up with a rope around the neck your ownself!"

"But Hardy's gotta stand fair trial," Coulter bleated, shivering in his sweaty socks. "What's the all-fired hurry? A day in court an' judge an' jury'll give sanction. All legal-like!"

A contemptuous murmur overrode his protest. "We got more confidence in our own justice. An' if'n yuh know he's guilty, what does the judge's sayso matter?"

"Stand aside, Sheriff! We're movin' in!"

Where the hell was his deputy,

Coulter wondered. If ever a man needed back-up, it was now. Hadn't Snyder noticed the mayhem that was brewing in town? Most nights when he was off duty found him in the Scarlet Crescent saloon, where a lot of these galoots had been drinking up big if their breath and their bold talk were anything to go by.

Why hadn't Snyder hot-footed it along to the office to fill him in on the drastic developments before the rowdies had gotten around to coming busting in?

"Keys! Give us yuh keys, Sheriff!" The intruders had realised that the massive door to the cell block was locked.

With shaking fingers Coulter reached into his desk drawer.

★ ★ ★

Kyle Hardy heard the mounting ruckus outside the jailhouse many moments before his half-deaf jailer. Trouble afoot, but of what kind and for whom, he couldn't tell. He could only guess . . .

And the images that formed behind his craggy countenance were not pretty. A mob is an ugly thing with a life of its own, but no mind.

He patted the gun hidden below his pants belt. Well, he had six shots. That was something.

The disturbance outside grew closer. The tumult was approaching bedlam, though it was impossible to pick out any individual words. Kyle's suspicions and fears magnified along with the sounds.

He got to his feet, stepped up to the heavy steel-barred door and rattled it on its hinges.

"Hey! Old-timer!"

Seth Hetrick jerked out of his slumber again.

"Goddamnit, mister! Yuh got ants in yuh pants or some — " He broke off, his watery eyes boggling, mouth agape. The prisoner was covering him with a long-barrelled Colt.

"Where'd ynh git that?" he quavered.

"No mind, old man. An' get them hands clear o' that gut-blaster, y'understand, or I'll plug you!"

Though not the scholarly type, Hetrick was a firm subscriber to the sixteenth-century proverb that discretion was the better part of valour. He hoisted his bent old arms well clear of the weaponry.

"That's jest fine. Now step up real close an' turn around."

Not knowing what to expect but in fear of his life, the oldster complied. Kyle tugged powerfully at the ring of keys attached to his pants by a belt loop. They came free with a rip.

Kyle could now hear argumentative voices through the door to the sheriffs office. Even his aged jailer must be able to hear them. Had he left it too late to make his play? What kind of hornet's nest did he face out there?

Still covering Hetrick with the Colt, Kyle shoved the key left-handed into the lock of his cell door, turned it and let himself loose.

At the same time he heard a double report of gunfire in the sheriffs office. Inside the building it reverberated like cannon blasts.

Kyle's gaze shifted momentarily and Hetrick, maybe jolted into rashness by the two shots, made an unexpected scramble for the ten-gauge.

★ ★ ★

When Coulter's hand emerged from his desk drawer, it was clutching not keys but a Smith and Wesson. But whether it was because he didn't have the nerve, or whether he was just too slow, he didn't get the chance to fire first.

The man with the drawn Colt, though not expecting trickery, drilled him through the shoulder. Coulter's trigger finger convulsed and his revolver span, exploding, from his suddenly numbed hand.

"Yuh asked fer it, yuh stupid fat

bastard!" the shooter roared.

Then it was all on. The taste for blood was whetted. The cries of rage and frustration knew no bounds.

A great bull of a waddie, with riding boots heavily reinforced to hold a stirrup under the instep, swung a mighty foot at the door to the cells. The stout door took the punishment, but with a second kick, the jamb splintered and the door crashed in.

★ ★ ★

Seth Hetrick was a peaceable man, not given to the impetuosity that might see a younger buck going off half-cocked. His fighting days, when he'd lived with nerves on a hair-trigger, were long done.

But no sooner had he snatched up his shotgun than the door that divided him from unknown carnage without was subjected to a thunderous and alarming assault.

Hetrick's big gun wavered, pointing

in every direction at once, it seemed to Kyle — making it impossible for him to snap off a disarming shot with his donated Colt. And at this stage, though aggrieved, he didn't feel disposed to having his guard's death on his hands.

So when the solid timber door fell in, narrowly missing beheading Hetrick and smashing down in a great cloud of dust and frame splinters beside him, the old man was primed to let rip with his hellish armament.

The scattergun went off with a flare of orange flame and a thunderclap that left eardrums muffled.

The buckshot carved a bloody arc of horrific red perforation across the barrel-like chest of the door-kicker. He crumpled with a scream on to his knees, before keeling over in a dead heap.

The bloodthirsty mob, splattered with the stuff of its own nightmarish lust, fell back into the sheriffs office, seeking what cover it could behind desks and cabinets. The room was filled with moans and wails of the injured and the stench of cordite.

Kyle realised that his erstwhile opponent had become, perforce, his unexpected ally, and that they were standing shoulder to shoulder, each gun in hand, ranked against the marauders.

It was a stand-off. The would-be lynchers had the pair of them bottled in. But if they made a move toward the jailhouse doorway, they knew they would be cut down.

"This fight ain't yours, Hetrick," a mob ringleader called. "Why don't yuh throw that thing down an' come out here? We don't aim to kill *you*."

"The hell it ain't my fight!" wheezed Hetrick. "I didn't start the shootin' an' it looks t'me like one o' you hellions has plugged the sheriff."

"Jeezus! We gotta man dead. We're bein' *lenient*, old man. If that jasper yuh've let out an' armed tries to walk outa here, yuh're both dead men."

"Mebbe," Kyle cut in. "But there'll be plenty of you who'll go to Boot Hill along with us."

How long the impasse would have endured, with Kyle and Hetrick holed up, was never put to the test. All at once a chilling cry interrupted from the street beyond the darkened courthouse alley outside.

"Fire! Fire!"

10

The Longest Night

VERITY TYLER sat on the front verandah of the Diamond-T ranch-house with her father. Neither had said anything for a long time. But it was a companionable silence beneath the vast, star-sprinkled black dome of the sky.

Her father was never a good sleeper. He said the inactivity forced upon him by his health didn't allow a man to have an honest night's rest. But Verity knew that were the truth to be admitted, any greater exertion than he customarily took would have killed him. And then on top of the physical pains, there were the worries and the frustrations wheeling around them like waiting buzzards eager to claim their helpless prey . . .

Tonight it was no wonder Old John couldn't sleep. Verity, though born and bred to be a frontierswoman with all the resourcefulness and fortitude that implied, was similarly afflicted. It wasn't every day a son and a brother was buried. She'd done her crying and was dry-eyed now, yet her sore-rimmed eyes kept straying to the new mound that was Tom's grave. The unweathered, fresh white timber of the cross she'd fashioned marked it clearly in the starlight at the edge of the silver beeches.

It was the longest night of her life.

"Don't reckon he's acomin' back," Old John grumbled suddenly into the dark silence.

Verity was startled in a way that made her flesh creep, because her own thoughts at that moment had been on her dead brother. But she quickly realised that her pa was talking about Kyle Hardy. She made out that the black silhouette of his head was turned in the direction of the trail out

151

to Sweetwater Springs.

Indeed, her own thoughts had been curiously divided, so that the sense of loss she felt had some other subtle content beyond their untimely bereavement.

"He was just a drifter," she sighed. "Like they said, another saddle-bum."

"Too bad of 'im, buildin' up folks' hopes like that. Still, what does a man need when he's footloose? Jest his hoss, a place to unroll his bed, an' a dollar or two for his next spot o' grub."

"I thought he might have been searching for something more," Verity commented with a depth of perception that seemed presumptuous for a mere girl who'd seen but eighteen summers.

"Nah. He had all he'd need." John Tyler catalogued Kyle Hardy's ostensible wealth with a wistful envy. "A strong body in its prime. Saddle, blanket and bridle. A bedroll back in town, I guess. Boots and spurs and guns."

Verity tossed her head. "Well, I don't

152

want to think about it," she said. "He was kind and helpful to me, but he's abandoned us after all."

It was a statement she didn't want to believe. Maybe it had something to do, too, with why she'd sat out here with her father all these dark hours. It wasn't just his company or being too comfortable to move from the rawhide chairs. She'd been hoping Kyle Hardy would still come riding back, as he'd promised.

But then it was better, somehow, to believe that the rugged-faced stranger had changed his mind than that he'd fallen foul of the same vile enemies who'd so ruthlessly and brutally disposed of Tom.

"It's more than we c'n handle now, child."

This time Verity followed the shift of her father's thoughts instantly. Their chances of holding out against the land-hungry Bart Brannigan were less than zero.

The Diamond-T was just about

the only worthwhile small spread left in the valley. Her father had been here early, before Brannigan, and had carved himself out a modest but well endowed holding with lush pastures and convenient watering-holes.

Then Brannigan had arrived and, once he was wifeless, had embarked on what could only be called a rampage of expansion, gobbling up into his Triple-Z spread every parcel of territory he could.

"Losing his wife triggered a kinda fever in his brain that was never cured," her father would say. It was a benevolent explanation for a man whose actions didn't entitle him to benevolence. Verity saw Brannigan's motivation as plain greed.

The nastiness was reflected in the son, Lance Brannigan, too. Self-centred and spoilt, Lance's interests were fancy clothes, booze and women.

Verity had never told her father how Lance, then about seventeen, had cornered her once behind the

154

schoolhouse in Sweetwater Springs. She was only ten at the time, but long-limbed and pretty with the grace of a young deer.

He'd told her a bird was lying hurt under the schoolhouse, a built-up frame structure. Could she crawl under and bring it out?

Trusting and willing, she'd done as she was bid. Except there was no bird to rescue and Lance had plunged into the dark space after her and pushed up her sensible homespun skirt and torn her cotton petticoat. She'd been lucky. A vigorous thrust with her school-shoed foot had caught him dead-centre in the groin. He writhed in sudden agony, his lust miraculously squelched, and her slimness enabled her to wriggle free and nimbly make her escape.

Even in those days, eight years ago, people feared the Brannigan power and influence. An intelligent child, beyond her years in perception and without a mother, Verity decided to hold her tongue about the incident. She told no one. But she'd still had nightmares in which her vengeful father stormed off to the Tiple-Z with a shotgun to deal to the depraved hooligan only to be bloodily cut down himself by a posse of desperadoes riding for Bart Brannigan.

Needless to say, she'd ever since given Lance Brannigan the widest of berths.

But now her father was admitting that the task of running the Diamond-T in defiance of the Brannigan overtures would prove too much for them.

The end he'd fended off so stubbornly and for so long was in sight.

"I mean to go down fightin', Verity, an' it ain't proper I should ask a young woman to stick it out with me, even my own daughter. Mebbe tomorrer yuh should pack up your things an' take the stage to the railhead, go back East to your ma's folks."

It was too dark for her to see, but she could imagine the animation in the half-live face, the fire of anger burning bright in his right eye.

Verity said softly, "No, Pa, I'm staying. The Diamond-T has been my home all my life and I want no other. It's my fight as much as yours."

"Waal, I knew yuh'd say it, gal, an' I guess I can't make yuh go. But it's gonna be an ugly business."

Verity hoped her father couldn't see the shudder she suppressed. She knew that should it come her fate in the hands of the Brannigan mob would not be pretty.

She'd heard the whispered stories of how the Triple-Z riffraff, including Bart's son, had forced themselves on the women whose men they'd beaten and sometimes killed. Largely, those women had accepted their lot, it appeared. For what else could they do, the reasoning went. The shame was not one to be paraded through a snickering, frontier-town court. It seemed to Verity that no matter how one tried to lead a civilised life, the American West ultimately dragged one down to the level of the scum who degraded it.

But she silently vowed she would draw her last breath, kill herself if need be, before she let Lance Brannigan lay his bestial hands on her. That one small taste of his handling all those years before had been as much as she could bear.

If only the big, capable stranger who'd sprung up from nowhere hadn't deserted them just as quickly. Then, she felt, they might have stood a chance.

She tried to put the might-have-beens out of her mind. But Kyle Hardy continued to dominate her thoughts. She wondered where he might be now, with his soothing, reassuring drawl and his powerful frame suggesting strength and stability. He'd only been one man, but for a few brief hours he'd given her faith that the Diamond-T just might overcome the odds.

A hint of moisture re-entered her eyes and a lump formed in her throat.

★ ★ ★

"Fire! Fire!"

The cry was one of the most dreaded to be heard in a settlement like Sweetwater Springs. The various edifices had a high content of combustible material in them. The sun-dried clapboard sheathing and other lumber would go up like tinder. And the town's pioneers had clustered their buildings together, many with only the narrowest of noisome alleys to divide them from their neighbours. In times when attack by Apache Indians was a constant threat, this rudimentary pattern of town planning made them easier to defend. But it also made the spread of fire a potentially rapid and totally devastating process.

When the mob that packed in and around Sheriff Coulter's office heard the alarm, it was instantly polarised into two factions.

The townies, who had been the mob's biggest component, made a surge for exits that would allow them to come to grips with the new

159

emergency. Even those who'd looked to be stinko displayed an alacrity to be in other places that astonished Kyle Hardy, who'd been holding them at bay with his donated Colt and the help of his shotgun-toting jailer, Seth Hetrick.

That left the inner core of ringleaders. These were the imported, hardbitten types who lived by the gun and whom Kyle had always picked as his real and most formidable opponents. They were on the Brannigan payroll for sure and in on the clever scheme to put him out of the way.

But at least the unexpected exodus went a long way toward evening the fight.

"Hey! Hold it, yuh jugheads! We got business to finish!" bawled one of the gunnies.

"The devil with that, mister! We'd be jugheads to stay an' lose our livelihoods!" retorted a red-nosed storekeeper.

"Reckon so!" cried another voice amid a general chorus of assent.

Hetrick, hard of hearing and maybe

perplexed at seeing so many supposed parties to the sheriffs shooting hightailing it, bowled forward on his bandy legs, waving the ten-gauge.

"Hold hard, yuh blasted coyotes! Thar's — "

Twin stabs of flame and the roar of six-guns ended the oldster's attempted intervention. The stock of the shotgun was shattered, but before it span out of his hands, its muzzle flared and a spreading blast of unaimed shot smashed holes in flesh and the far wall. Hetrick was history — and so was one of his killer's *compadres*.

Hetrick went down almost silently with just a wheezy sigh; the other man screamed shrilly, knowing gut-searing agony and terrible fear before he died.

Under cover of the fresh violence, Kyle took his chance and leapt out of the jailhouse doorway and behind the less-than-ideal protection of the sheriffs desk. Coulter was still groaning and moaning and clutching his shoulder where a widening bloodstain reddened his shirt. He was out of the fight. No threat. And huddled down here Kyle was less hemmed in and several steps closer to freedom.

"That wasn't necessary, goddamnit," Kyle growled at the gunnie who'd cut down Hetrick.

The man jeered. "It was self-defence, yuh do-good sticky bill! Another move an' yuh'll get your'n the same way."

"I don't reckon so. Anyone else shoots, an' you'll be first to go with me!" Kyle levelled the Colt and braced his right wrist with his left hand.

From his new vantage point, Kyle could see that the fire was a hummer, its glow lighting the sky and smoke billowing into the courthouse alley. In the silence that now fell, he could hear the crackle of flames, too, above a pandemonium of frantic yelling.

Four Brannigan henchmen still faced him, irons drawn. It was stalemate again, none of them daring to shoot first.

And again it was from outside that the situation took its next unexpected twist. Smoke was swirling into the office in choking eddies from the town's streets.

"Stay here long enough an' you'll all be burned up long afore you get to hell," Kyle was telling the gunnies when a tall, black-garbed figure in a flat-crowned hat loomed up silently out of the black clouds in the open doorway to the alley.

"Get me outa here," whined Coulter.

"Aw, shut your trap, or we'll end your misery an' blame the saddle-bum," a gunnie said.

The first the Brannigan four knew about the newcomer was when he ducked under the lintel into the office, guns rudely announcing his arrival without preliminary.

Two of the four were dead without seeing their ruthless executioner; the other two glimpsed the lean, hatchet-faced gunfighter Jules Despard.

They were swivelling round from

163

Kyle Hardy, bringing their shooters to bear on this new enemy. Then two more shots were ringing into the echoes of the previous and they were clutching their bellies.

They died with eyes staring wide in horrified amazement, startled oaths frozen on their lips.

Kyle's heart hammered against his ribs. Was his own life the next on the line? The Colt butt was wet with sweat in his palm. So far, incredibly, he hadn't had to fire the unknown weapon in this savage bloodbath.

But he wouldn't hesitate if Despard turned his irons as much as one degree toward him.

11

Despard Shows his Hand

"TAKE it easy, pard'ner," Despard said. "It'd be a great pity to have t'salivate yuh now." The words creaked from his throat like the rolling of an unoiled wagon wheel.

Kyle didn't relax his guard. "Since when've I been a pard'ner of a hired killer?" he asked. He was searching the gaunt gun-slick's face. But the man's eyes were like globs of quicksilver. Cold. Hard. Expressionless.

Despard made a noise that might have been a laugh. "Yuh're the one they calls Hardy, ain't yuh? Wal, lissen, yuh would of bin buzzard chow by now if it wasn't fer me."

Spots of colour burned on Kyle's craggy cheekbones. He'd remembered the figure he'd seen lurking in the shadows out back of his cell.

He hefted the Colt. "Were you the *hombre* that chucked this through the bars?" he asked.

"The very same, mister."

Kyle recognised his indebtedness and was far from happy about it. None of this added up.

"Look, Despard," he said, reaching a swift decision, "there's fire spreadin' out there. I got questions aplenty but the palaver can wait. We gotta get ourselves out. An' this jackass of a sheriff likewise — "

Kyle gestured toward Coulter slumped in pale-faced misery behind his desk.

"Nope! There's others c'n do that, pard," Despard replied impassively. "If Coulter can't make it under his own steam, he stays till they comes. Savvy?"

Despard wasn't a man you could hold a debate with at the best of times. Kyle listened to the rising ruckus in Main Street. He smelled the eye-watering fumes of a blaze that might even now be creeping toward them, cutting them off, sealing their doom as surely as any slug from a .45.

"All right," he said at last, irritably. "No more gabbin'. Let's take ourselves off while we've got the chance."

"Now yuh's talkin' sense, Hardy. Once that fire's doused, yuh're a marked man for sairtain. An' yuh an' me's got business to do someplace else."

That jolted Kyle. "Business? I ain't goin' no place with you. I may owe you a debt, Despard, but I don't ride with bounty hunters!"

"Not even to save the Diamond-T? Wal, stagger me! I thought yuh'd taken a shine to that green Tyler kid's spunky sister."

Despard was sure of his man. As he spoke, he holstered his twin Colts and confidently strode out the door on his long legs.

Kyle grabbed up his own gun rig from where Coulter had tossed it on a pine and brass chest behind his desk and followed the tall gunfighter.

"Whadya mean, Despard?" he called after him.

All at once new fears had clutched at his heart.

★ ★ ★

Coulter heard the footsteps of the two outsiders vanish rapidly into the blanketing smoke that was sweeping through the alley and starting to fill his office.

Between them they'd brought hell to his town. They'd destroyed a cosy set-up and now they were leaving him to die.

Due to his loss of blood he'd been hovering in and out of full consciousness for several minutes and he'd heard only parts of their cryptic conversation. But to his hazy understanding it appeared obvious they were in cahoots. Maybe they'd been so from the outset.

Carrion! Bastards!

He struggled to haul his flabby body

on to his feet. He had to get to the medicine chest; he was bleeding like a stuck pig from his shoulder and urgently needed a pad of wadding to staunch it. Then he had to get out of here before the courthouse building, too, took fire!

Suddenly he heard a key grating in the locked door that led to the adjacent courtroom proper, where Sweetwater Springs staged its trials.

Thank God! Help was at hand.

It was Izzy Snyder. The gangling deputy burst into the room, head thrust forward on his scrawny neck, eyes goggling at the carnage.

"Judas! What's bin goin' on in here, Coulter?"

The sheriff moaned. "Despard — gave Hardy a gun, busted him out. Here, help me, will yuh?"

Snyder was deaf to his request. "The lynch mob, ain't they fixed that saddle-bum?" he demanded.

Coulter's mouth twisted. "Naw, shot me instead, the scum."

169

"An' then what? Why ain't they dealt to Hardy?"

"Didn't have a chance, I tell yuh," the sheriff gasped. "Despard shot 'em up. Them that hadn't gone to fight the fire. I'm sick to m'guts with the whole passel of 'em."

Snyder scowled, his face congested darkly with rage. Beneath his drooping moustache, his mouth contorted in a venomous sneer.

He was disgusted with how things had panned out. This didn't fit in with his plans at all. He wanted Hardy dead, to satisfy the all-powerful Brannigans and at the same time discredit the sheriff so he could take his place.

But Coulter hadn't gone along with a nonexistent lynching, which would have been a dereliction of his duty. Nor in opposing its promotion had he gotten himself killed — merely injured.

At the end of the day, when sobriety and sanity restored themselves, he might even come out looking like a wounded hero. With Hardy still alive, there would be no guilt feelings to silence the tongues that might oppose Coulter's removal.

No need for a scapegoat either.

Coulter bleated testily, "Fer Chrissakes, are yuh gonna give me a hand with this busted shoulder or just stand thar gawping?"

"Sure, Sheriff. Let's take a closer look-see."

Snyder moved in on him and saw his eyes screw up with pain as he settled back in his chair, leaning his head aside to give him unrestricted access to the bullet wound.

The smell of the freshly spilled blood was strong in Snyder's nostrils, and when he swallowed even his saliva had a saline taint. An exhilaration throbbed through his veins as he seized his opportunity.

His hand dipped to his hip and he drew his six-gun smoothly with a surprisingly steady hand. What kind of attention was going to be paid to one more corpse at the Sweetwater Springs funeral parlour?

It was so safe; so easy.

The fleshy lids over Coulter's piggy eyes fluttered open. He saw Snyder point the gun at close range to the soggy wet patch centred on his injured shoulder. He screamed then in sudden, dawning comprehension.

His deputy intended treachery.

"Yuh bastard, Snyder! Yuh stinkin' bastard!"

The gun blasted shatteringly in his ears. And then, with shocking immediacy, a red-hot ball seemed to drive down into his chest, tearing him up, and all his senses were flying apart at great speed into a dense blackness.

His dying brain sent three last words through the blood bubbling into his throat.

"Yuh-murdered-me!"

Unmoved, Snyder quickly removed himself from the scene. He still had other fish to fry. And first he had to catch them.

* * *

The leaping glare from blazing buildings lit up Sweetwater Springs like a fireworks display. It dwarfed the feeble pools of yellow lamplight that spilled from the doorways and windows of untouched portions of the town, hastily vacated by their night-bird clientele and the storekeepers and tradespeople who, with their families, had rushed to isolate the spreading flames.

Jules Despard made tracks purposefully through the black smoke and the shadows.

Kyle Hardy ducked along after him. He was in two minds about his release from jail. He'd escaped being railroaded on to the end of a hangnoose, but now he was a fugitive. Once the fire crisis was over, he imagined a posse would be recruited to come hunting him like an animal. There was no way he could return to the Diamond-T, heaping his new troubles on the Tylers'

173

bowed shoulders.

That galled him badly. And what was this hint that Despard had dropped about the Diamond-T needing saving? Were Verity and her father and their two sad apologies for a ranch crew under some new threat?

Being on the dodge would bring with it an impotence to respond to his deep desire to assist them. For long years, he'd led a careless style of life, doing as he chose, following his inclinations unfettered. But all this was going to be changed overnight. Did Sweetwater Springs have the telegraph? If so, the shot sheriff, or his assistants, could shortly be sending out the word, and his freedom to roam where he willed would be abruptly curtailed.

A price would be put on his head. The 'wanted' posters would come with his name on them, stark and black off the presses.

He had his friends and they weren't without influence, but they couldn't be seen dirtying their reputations by interfering in the slaying of a saloon whore.

Life would then degenerate into one never-ending extension of this flitting through the shadows, forever glancing over his shoulder, watching his back, not daring to rest in honest sleep, lest the rough hand of the law should signal his awakening and recapture.

Could he flee south, reach the Border, cross the Rio Grande into Mexico? Maybe. But was that where he wanted to be?

He had not murdered Maria Cortazzi. He was not a criminal. Yet this forcible running at the behest of an unscrupulous bounty hunter would surely condemn him in the eyes of all right-thinking communities.

The opinion of the law would be that he had proven his guilt in taking flight — dictated though flight had been by circumstances that to an impartial observer could be shown as entirely reasonable.

Somewhere along the backs of Main

Street came the crash of a collapsing roof. An explosion of golden sparks whirled high above the eddying pall of black smoke into a night sky flecked with distantly winking silver stars.

Despard cackled dryly. "Good, huh? Keeps 'em occupied."

"I dunno. Convenient maybe. Lucky . . ."

"Lucky nothing. Who d'yuh think set this stinkin' hole alight?"

"I might of guessed it. What's your game, Despard?"

"Yuh c'n call it a settlin' o' accounts."

"Who with? The citizens?"

"Nope. Most of 'em are brainless clods and sycophants."

"Who then?"

"Their bosses, the Brannigans mostly."

"I thought you was doin' business for 'em."

"Was, is right, mister. But these things cost an' they got kinda reluctant to cough up outa their money-bags. No one cheats on me, y'understand?"

176

Kyle nodded slowly, getting the picture. "I'm beginnin' to."

"That Lance thinks he's hell in hand-tooled boots, but he's gonna be wettin' his fancy pants afore I'm finished with him. An' his old man drew a sneak gun on me when I went to c'llect m' dues. Blew smoke in m' face from some damn' poisonous black cheroot an' all." Despard's face split in a death's-head grin. "He's gonna be real mad when he larns most o' the property he holds a lien over has gone up in real black smoke!"

Kyle chewed his lip. Something was nagging at him, but right then his mind was in too much of a whirl for him to put his finger on it. "This still don't explain why you've sprung me out of the cooler," he said.

"I figgered I could do with the extra gun power an' you an' me are kinda nat'ral allies, seein's how yuh've linked up with the Diamond-T an' the Brannigans have got it in fer you an' the Tylers both. They reckon they got yuh hog-tied, pard. Yuh're gonna take the blame, see?"

"Quit talkin' in goddam riddles!" Kyle rapped, heedless that his raised voice would betray their furtive passage through the back alleys of town.

"Don't get your dander up, mister. My fight is your'n, like I say. Them big-shot cow prodders are makin' their move on the Diamond-T before sun-up. I heerd their plans. They're gonna kill ev'ry man-jack of 'em and take care o' the gal the same ways as they fixed up that saloon whore."

"Holy God!"

The sudden rush of blood and the pounding of Kyle's pulses brought fresh pain to his gun-bruised head.

"Yeah. The Brannigans are gonna put it around the saddle-bum the Tylers foolishly hired — namely y'self — had gone clean off his head, murdered them each, then lit off t' town. But the taste for blood an' dirty sport still gripped 'im, the tale goes, so he took his savag'ry out on Lance, Hoffman and Maria."

Before sun-up. The Brannigans' foul intentions and the grim deadline filled Kyle with horror.

"We've gotta hit the trail faster 'n fast!" he cried fiercely.

"My own conclusion likewise, pard. Yuh'll be pleased to know I c'llected that sorrel o' your'n from the livery stables. I seen yuh hitch it up b'hind the Tyler buckboard. It's waitin' along with my own cayuse jest down the street apiece."

Far from dragging his feet, Kyle Hardy was now more than anxious to co-operate with Despard on whatever intervention he had in mind.

But Kyle's agitated voice had been picked up on as they scuttled through the darkened, smoky streets. Before they could race like the wind out of town another deadly confrontation lay before them.

12

'Your Number's Up!'

IZZY SNYDER was a worried man. Lief Coulter was disposed of neatly. To his complete satisfaction. The sheriff had already been shot in the fracas surrounding the escape of the prisoner Hardy. Would it be any great surprise when he was found dead? Snyder didn't think so.

But Hardy's freedom was another matter.

The Brannigans would be highly displeased. The book might not be so conveniently closed on the death of Maria Cortazzi, in which he himself had been implicated. Had Hardy seen him or Lance upstairs at the *Paloma Blanca*? He thought not. But he couldn't be sure.

And what the hell was Jules Despard

180

up to — or had that damned fool Coulter been mistaken in his spluttered accusation?

Snyder, like most everyone else hereabouts, had viewed the gunfighter's coming to Sweetwater Valley with a healthy respect. Not so, apparently, the Brannigans. It was on their invitation, he was privileged to understand, that Despard had made his entry. The prospect of seeing the fresh-faced Tom Tyler blasted to kingdom-come by the macabre professional gun-slick had tickled young Lance's fancy. He had strange tastes and warped pleasures did that rich man's son.

Snyder hoped Coulter had been wrong and that the spectacular heeling of the Tylers hadn't blown up in the Brannigans' faces.

He shivered a little. He didn't relish the possibility of coming up against Despard, but it was important that Hardy should be found quickly and disposed of.

So now he stalked the streets to that

end. Colt drawn. Ears cocked.

It hadn't been many minutes since he'd witnessed the storming of the jailhouse by the lynch mob and the first shots had rung out. Still fewer minutes had elapsed since a crazed Emilio Vicente — who'd been unable to join the mob and bring himself face to face with the callous killer of his beautiful Maria — had stumbled in frantic haste down the middle of Main Street proclaiming the outbreak of fire in his deserted *cantina*.

Therefore, Hardy could not have gone far. But if Despard had indeed freed him, the flight could have been prepared, with mounts stashed nearby.

Snyder took the direction he thought most likely to be favoured by his quarry — away from the fire, toward the trail out of town. He slipped cautiously from shadow to shadow. Eventually, he was rewarded.

"Quit talkin' in goddam riddles!"

Kyle Hardy's harsh demand carried to him through the darkness, followed by the terse mutters of conversation he couldn't decipher. But he knew that other voice. No one else but Jules Despard sliced his words out like a crosscut saw.

So it was true.

Despard was blazing a trail of his own, paying no mind to the interests of the Sweetwater Valley big boss man!

Snyder smiled slyly to himself. Maybe the situation wasn't so scary after all. Back-shoot these two clever bastards and Brannigan will owe me one helluva bonus, he told himself.

The prospect of plaudits and cold hard cash emboldened him. He would be the lawman who'd taken out Jules Despard, a thorn in the flesh of a hundred territories, a bounty hunter who walked the fine line between what the law allowed and what it didn't. Cocking a snoot at it. This time, in aiding and abetting an accused murderer, Despard had slipped up.

He had every right to gun them both down like dogs.

Why should he have let Despard's reputation give him the heebie-jeebies? At bottom he was only a flesh-and-blood man. He wasn't as goddamned smart as they made out. He was making a big mistake in dabbling in the Hardy matter for starters. Now he, Snyder, was going to make Despard's mistake an even bigger one. The *biggest*.

All he had to do now was move in and fire the shots. It was one against two, but that wouldn't matter. He had surprise on his side and he'd be careful to keep back in the shadows. His confidence quickened with his heartbeat.

On the outskirts of the town, his two quarries took more risks, striding less circumspectly across open patches of moonlight. This far out, Sweetwater Springs was more sparsely built anyway.

Scurrying after them, Snyder saw two saddled horses nibbling the coarse grass growing at the foot of a white-painted picket fence outside the church.

A high-standing streaky dun and a sorrel.

These were his men all right. Snyder felt good, excited. Like he'd felt when he'd dealt to Coulter, knowing it was going to be easy and all so perfect. It wasn't incumbent on him to make his presence known, but what the hell? A deputy didn't often get to call a bounty hunter and know he had to win. His Colts were already in his fists, the hammers back. The hot blood was racing through his veins.

"Your number's up, Despard!"

The exultant cry and the firing of his guns rang out, the second so hard on the heels of the first that nothing seemed to separate them.

But the tall man in black had dropped to the dust in a blur before the heavy .45 slugs reached him. And he shot back daringly from the thigh, his fire unerringly fixed on the muzzle flames that betrayed Snyder's presence in the shadows.

If nothing spaced Snyder's threat

from his gun-blasts, Despard's single shot was so close to them that it blotted them, cheating them of echoes.

Kyle's sorrel shied nervously, adding its whinny to the dramatic din.

Snyder never had time to ponder the recklessness of opening his mouth in that last stupid threat. He was lying dead, face down in the dirt, his Colts still smoking, when Despard rearranged his long limbs into upright stance and said casually to Kyle Hardy, "I knew he was thar agunnin' all the time. Sucker!"

He stooped to pick up his flat-crowned hat and dusted it off.

Kyle was astounded by it all. It was the slickest piece of counter-shooting he'd ever seen. And Kyle was no slouch with a gun himself. Either Despard's senses were honed to infallibility by experience, or he had supernatural instincts.

Whatever, he was glad his unlikely ally had been watching their butts.

He crossed to the fallen man,

knowing from his stillness he had to be a corpse. "Snyder! The deputy!"

"Don't let it worry yuh, Hardy. He'd pulled his irons an' he weren't tryin' t' make no arrest. 'Sides, he's jest another o' them Brannigan stooges."

The claim confirmed what Kyle already suspected. And it was no time to discuss the allegiances of a dead man. The name Brannigan refocused all his concerns on the murderous threat that hung over Verity Tyler, her father and the hands of the Diamond-T.

Abruptly he turned to the horses, halted briefly to tighten the cinch, then put his foot in the sorrel's stirrup and swung up into the saddle.

There'd been enough delay. Behind them the flickering light from burning buildings was being replaced by a dark pall of ashy smoke.

"Let's ride!" he yelled.

Dust spurted beneath the sorrel's hoofs as it leaped forward to the touch of his heels.

★ ★ ★

They'd quickly cleared town limits and kneed their mounts into a lasting pace on the trail to the Diamond-T. Neither horse was particularly fresh, though Kyle's was more so than Despard's.

Even a wild gallop, had it been possible or wise, would not have satisfied Kyle. He was in the grip of an anxiety totally foreign to the easy-going ways he'd allowed to creep up on him and become second nature these past several years.

At one time back in his past he'd been subject day-to-day to the rigorous discipline of army life. But the goals that had set had never seemed as vital and pressing as the one before him now.

In recent times, he'd followed the free and uncommitted life of the roving cowpuncher. Till it had palled on him. Then he'd looked for purpose. Given it, he'd pursued it to the point where today he'd been balked by murder and false witness and slung into a small-town jail.

But it wasn't that curtailing of his assignment that had wrought the profound change in his attitude these last few tumultuous hours. It was very blue eyes in a firm-chinned, sun-bronzed face that spoke of inner strength and loyalty and courage. He recognised with a wry sort of wonder that it was Verity Tyler, and the threat to her safety, that gripped him with something close to panic and galvanised him into action.

Despard suddenly spurted alongside him and leaned across and tugged at his horse's reins.

"Draw in!" he rasped.

"For God's sake, Despard! What are you doin'?"

A burst of anger flooded through Kyle at the thought of his companion trying to slow their progress. But then he, too, heard the faint rumbling sound across the rolling prairie behind them.

He reined in, sitting up tall in the

saddle, stiffening. The protest died on his wind-dried lips.

"Riders!" Despard ground out. "The Triple-Z in force an' on fresher broncs than our'n."

Kyle figured they'd been going for about ten minutes and that they were still some miles from the Tyler spread.

"We'll be overtaken," he said, his craggy face grim with concern.

It sounded now like an army was pounding up behind them in the darkness.

Despard lifted a long arm and pointed to an outcrop of boulders off to their right across the grasslands. "Take cover, or we'll be outrun and overrun!" he said.

"But we've gotta warn the Diamond-T!"

"Not a chance. Keep on the trail an' yuh die to no purpose."

The gunfighter was right. The open range was no place for a showdown. They were just two against what sounded like a horde. Kyle thought

190

with a sick dismay that they possibly stood no chance of helping the Tylers at all. Their whole mission might be doomed to end in bloody folly.

He plunged his horse in the path of Despard's rangy dun and headed for the cluster of rocks.

Some of the boulders loomed big enough to conceal a horse and rider and there were more of them than it had seemed from the trail. Kyle put one between himself and the approaching horsemen and sat to await their passing.

The drumming noise grew louder, then the leaders of the pack swept into sight, a series of hell-bent shapes silhouetted against the silvery night sky.

Kyle thought he glimpsed the white sombrero of Lance Brannigan among the front runners.

Despard, too, was picking out familiar figures. He said, "The beefy feller on the black stallion is Big Bart hisself. Takin' a hand in his own dirty work, huh?"

Kyle remembered the talk he'd heard from Verity and at the Diamond-T ranch-house. "I understand he thinks the holding-out of the Diamond-T is a special score he has to settle with Old John Tyler personally. Apparently he's had a few fleas in his ears from that direction."

Despard swore. "Ain't nothin' to the score-settlin' I'm gonna do," he vowed. He slapped a gaunt hand on the warbag tied behind the cantle of his saddle. "That crowd's in fer a real shakin'."

The gunman sounded very sure of himself. Yet for all that Kyle couldn't see what the blazes they could do to save the Tylers.

"I'll think of somethin'," Kyle promised himself with muted vehemence. "Goddamnit, I jest have to!"

192

13

Under Attack

VERITY TYLER had retired to her room after her father finally decided he should hit the sack. The night chills had crept in on the verandah from the open range, carried by the breeze from the far mountains. Her father had noticed her shivers.

But Verity's mind was too active for sleep. Even after the creakings from her father's bed in the adjacent room had ceased, she herself was still awake.

She was mulling for the millionth time the strange behaviour of the man called Kyle Hardy when she heard riders approaching. Was Hardy returning after all? But this was the clatter of many hoofs, not the solitary clop of a lone drifter.

Why should there be night callers at

the Diamond-T?

Had Hardy gotten into some kind of trouble, and were these people bringing word? The Tylers had worries enough of their own, she thought, uncharacteristically cross.

Verity tossed aside her blankets and got up, hoping her father wouldn't be disturbed, because the horsemen outside were making no effort to arrive quietly. She hastily lit an oil lamp. There must be close to a dozen of them, she guessed, but her one smallish, high window didn't give any view of the entrance to the ranch buildings.

She quickly pulled on check shirt, jerkin and whipcord pants and stepped into halfboots. She did up only half the shirt buttons and was still buckling her belt when she hurried out to the front of the house.

Verity was no farther than the verandah when shots rang out from the bunkhouse without warning. Between the confusion of the arrivals' milling horses, she saw the Diamond-T foreman, Ned

Hammond, pitch out of the open bunkhouse door and roll into the dust at the bottom of its wooden steps.

One of the small army of horsemen let out a blood-chilling yahoo. "That's one of 'em fixed, fellers!" It was Lance Brannigan. The voice and the fancy sombrero were unmistakable.

Verity found herself shuddering. Whether from fear or horror or rage, she didn't know. Forcing the shakes out of her limbs through sheer effort of will, she turned back into the house. And collided with her father who had hobbled in a nightshirt to the door.

"Get back, Pa!" she blurted. "It's the Brannigans!"

"The bastards! I mighta known they'd try somethin'!"

But an overt attack! How would they explain this away? The amazing question was instantly crowded out of Verity's mind by the need to get arms for her own and her father's defence. Maybe they could still barricade themselves in and give an account

195

of themselves that would negate their attackers' audacity.

"We'll throw lead back at 'em, the swines! Beat 'em off!" her father barked stoutly.

No, Verity thought, as she thrust home the door bolts. It was next to hopeless. They were going to end up dead, and corpses couldn't tell the unbelievable tale of their passing. This was range war with all the coarse spite and the underhandedness she had learned to expect from the degenerate Lance Brannigan and his ruthless, bullying father. Might had become the only right.

"Gimme that Sharps, gal," her father ordered, grabbing the rifle she was pulling from a wall case. "What can stop buffalo can stop a Brannigan!"

Verity was tucking a small Smith and Wesson .32 into her belt when they heard excited shouts outside.

"We've flushed 'im out!"

"Thar he goes, the turkey!"

Gunfire rang out again. Then there

was a cry of pain and stumbling footfalls on the boards of the verandah, followed by a scrabbling and thumping on the door.

"For Christ's sake! I bin hit. Let me in!"

There was a chorus of taunting guffaws from the pleader's tormentors.

Old John Tyler lurched to the front of the house. "Quick, Verity! Unbolt the door. It's Ellison. We gotta let 'im in. With that missin' finger o' his, he ain't much of a hand at shootin'!"

"It's a trick!" Verity warned. "They'll force their way in."

"Jest let 'em try! I'll cover the door with the Sharps."

Reluctantly, but equally unable to ignore the desperate plight of their ranch-hand, Verity pulled at the bolts.

She was easing the door open when another shot crashed out, and the weight of Steve Ellison's body tumbled against the door, pushing it back. He shrieked with pain.

"They got my knee!"

He collapsed into a ragged heap on the stoop, then tried to drag himself in by his arms.

Old John saw the erratic trail of blood behind him. He knew Ellison couldn't make it without help. He was spent.

It was then the irascible, crippled rancher did a wild, incredibly foolhardy thing.

"Here, hold this, gal!"

He pushed the powerful Sharps into his daughter's hands, even though he must have known it was beyond her experience and strength to handle, and threw himself forward to grab a great bunch of Ellison's shirt back and add his own limited muscle to the man's fading strength.

The ranch-hand started to slide in, his breath coming in great pants, smearing blood across the boards behind him.

"No, Pa, don't!" Verity screamed from behind the door, realising her muleheaded father had exposed himself to deadly danger.

But it was too late.

She heard the sharp thunder crack of a rifle. Twice, in quick succession.

The first heavy bullet smacked audibly into her father's chest, felling him instantly on top of the half-dead Ellison, who jerked convulsively as he received the second.

"No . . . ! Oh, no!"

Sobbing, distraught beyond all reason, Verity dropped the Sharps and plunged back into her room, slamming the door and bracing a chair under the knob. In her right mind, she would have known she hadn't a hope of keeping anyone out.

Outside, the raiders were cheering their marksmanship and laughing and talking raucously, but the reverberations from the thunderous rifle reports had scarcely stopped ringing in her head before all hell broke loose.

* * *

199

Big Bart Brannigan shoved his Winchester back into the scabbard slung under his stirrup leathers and wheeled the black stallion. He was feeling mighty pleased with himself. It had given him great personal satisfaction to cut down Old John Tyler. The man had been a thorn in his flesh for as long as he'd been in Sweetwater Valley. His destruction would mark the beginning of a new era.

And it didn't hurt none, he told himself, for the hardbitten crew who rode for the Triple-Z to see the mettle of the man who paid their wages. It had been an easy shot, of course. The foolish old man had been a sitting duck. But no matter. These rannies would respect him just the same. You didn't buck Big Bart, or he'd deal to you, no pussyfooting around. That's the message they'd put around, and it'd help keep their mouths tight-shut when it came to any other stories they might be in a position to tell.

Big Bart was the power in the land.

"The gal's run back inside," said Lance Brannigan to no one in particular. His voice was thick and an unholy gleam lit his pale eyes. His face was shiny with sweat and excitement.

"Waal, she's the only one left, son," Bart said. He gave an evil chuckle. "Mebbe yuh should go in an' bring her out to join the party?"

The gunnie called Clem sniggered. "Mebbe Lance is figurin' on havin' a kinda *private* party."

There was general ribald laughter and Lance cleared his throat. "Sure, Clem, I reck'n I'll handle the bitch on my ownsome for starters. She owes me. It was her who dragged in that Hardy bum."

"Go to it, son," Bart gave the word. "Fix her real good. Remember, it's *Hardy* that's done all this — and he's gone plumb loco, right?"

More lewd hilarity was in order. Lance, preening himself facetiously, jumped down from the saddle and ran up the steps on to the verandah.

201

His life was saved at that point by the upright piece of four by four timber that formed one of the roof-supporting verandah posts. Barely two feet from his head, a heavy .44-40 slug whined past like a hornet and thunked into the post to the accompanying blast of a rifle.

Lance dived into the cover of the ranch-house.

It was the first of a volley of shots, and others were not so lucky.

★ ★ ★

"Gunfire!" Kyle Hardy exclaimed several minutes earlier, a sick knot gripping his gut. "We're gonna be too late!"

Despard had no understanding of the emotion that wracked him. "Never too late till yuh dead yuhself," he grated flatly. "Slow down. We gotta pick ourselves some cover."

They were inside the boundary line of the Diamond-T spread and cantered through a shallow stream, a swirl of ghostly luminance in the moonlight.

"There's some beeches makin' a copse an' linin' the ridge beyond the home-lot," Kyle remembered aloud.

"Sure," Despard responded, giving no credit. "Now quit jawin', will yuh? Ain't no sense in advertisin' we're here afore we've picked a couple off an' bettered the odds."

From the racket close ahead — there were more shots and a man's screams and incoherent pleading — it didn't seem likely to Kyle that the Brannigan gang was going to hear them. But Despard was his only ally. He was a man who didn't brook contradiction and Kyle couldn't afford to fall out with him at this juncture. Swallowing his impatience and his anxiety, he fell silent.

They trotted their horses at a pace that was infuriatingly sedate, then slowed them to little more than a walk as they approached the silver beeches that even from this different direction Kyle recognised as the distinctive backdrop to young Tom Tyler's fresh gave. The horses seemed grateful to plod, breath whistling harshly through distended nostrils, flanks and haunches saturated with lathered sweat.

Finally they dismounted and, leaving the horses ground-tied, flitted through the trees. But before leaving the beasts, they unshipped their carbines and Despard tugged a package from his warbag.

Kyle was horrified and dismayed at the scene that met his eyes. He looked slightly down and across from the trees and into the open space between the cluster of darkened ranch buildings, and saw the Brannigans whooping and hoorawing.

Three men were apparently dead.

One — the old foreman Hammond? — was curled up in the dust, a darkly ominous huddle a short way from the bunkhouse.

The other two were in the doorway to the ranch-house, dimly visible in the weak reflected light from a lamp he supposed to be set down some way back inside. One was John Tyler for sure. The other he assumed to be Ellison.

Lance Brannigan had just dropped from his horse and was swaggering toward the two bodies.

Where is Verity? The question hammered in Kyle's head.

"What are we waiting for?" came Despard's harsh whisper from somewhere in the shadows to his right.

Kyle snatched up his Winchester and levered a shell into the breech, raising the carbine's butt to his shoulder in the same movement and drawing a bead on his chosen target — Lance Brannigan.

Boom!

The crack of the Winchester was almost eardrum-bursting. And to Kyle's disgust he saw his shot waste itself in the veradah post, and Lance Brannigan diving into the ranch-house where he was quickly lost to sight. He jerked another shell into the breech and picked another target.

Despard fired non-stop, squinting down the barrel of his carbine, slinging his shots hard after each other at his selected quarry till it fell, whereupon with cold efficiency he'd swing the foresight around till it aligned with another hapless victim and he was set to repeat the deadly process. When he'd fired eleven times, he dipped into a black coat pocket and slid back into denser cover to reload the magazine.

Kyle, too, got into the rhythm and pumped shot after shot in quick succession into the surprised hardcases.

Strangled cries rent the air and bodies toppled from saddles with dead and heavy thumps to the ground.

The black stallion whinnied shrilly in fright. It reared up on its hind legs, eyes wide, white and rolling, front hoofs threshing air. Bart Brannigan wrestled to regain control of the panicking beast.

"We've bin bushwhacked!" he bawled, fit to bust a gut.

He was almost unable to credit that they'd been caught with their pants down; that there could be anyone alive in Sweetwater Valley who'd be brazen enough to interfere.

His purposeless, angry bellow did nothing to calm the stallion. Whether he lost his equilibrium or whether he was thrown by the startled horse, it was impossible for Kyle to judge. But his bulky, bull-necked body hurtled to the dust, where flashing hoofs missed him by a hairbreadth.

Brannigan saw his gang had been reduced around him to a mere four men, only one of whom was still on his horse.

The horseman, trying futilely to return the fire of their assailants, gestured with his Colt towards the puffs of gunsmoke that indicated Kyle's and Despard's hiding places in the beeches.

"The bastards are in them trees someplace, boss! More than one o'the stinkin' polecats!"

"Get under cover!" Brannigan shrieked, rolling clear of his stallion's stamping, iron-shod hoofs. "Ain't no way we c'n fight back out in the open!"

"It sure as all get out looks thataway!"

The range boss figured the closest and most complete protection between the ranch-house and the copse was back of the shed where the Diamond-T buckboard was kept. He ran for it. Pain knifed through his bruised and jarred body in a dozen places, and another Winchester slug kicked up the dust behind his boot heels.

"Save yuh bullets till we c'n make 'em count!" he spluttered to his followers. He was red-faced with apoplexy.

The four men miraculously reached safety with him, though the man still on horseback had to abandon his petrified mount to do so.

Brannigan now grinned crookedly and hefted his six-shooter. "They try an' flush us outa here an' they get a dose of hot lead! Mebbe Lance c'n get a bead on them from the house likewise, an' we got the gal hostage.

The game ain't over yet . . . not by a long ways!

"Ten Double-Eagles bonus fer the *hombre* that kills one o'them sonofabitches!"

14

Comanche Devilry

JULES DESPARD put aside the smoking Winchester with a curse of disgust.

"Mister Big Bart Brannigan runnin' to save his ass!" he snorted. "Hold your fire, pard, they ain't gonna show their heads agen in a hurry."

Kyle Hardy was amazed at the devastation their surprise retaliation had wrought. No fewer than eight new bodies were strewn in front of the Diamond-T ranch-house.

He frowned. "We ain't outa the woods yet, Despard. Make one move toward that blamed shed an' one of them hellions is gonna pop up and blast our heads off!"

"Yuh suggestin' we back out an' quit?" probed Despard.

210

Kyle sensed the question was intended to goad.

"Nope," he responded succinctly.

He mused a moment, uncertain how much he should say to this inhuman killing engine who was his comrade-in-arms. Then he added, "Not while we still ain't seen what's become o' Miss Tyler. An' I reckon it's a damn' shame we didn't pot either o' them Brannigans. They ain't jest mean — they're evil."

Kyle realised that his greatest, most depressing, fear was that the Brannigan gang had killed Verity Tyler along with the rest of the unfortunate inhabitants of the Diamond-T. But what had Lance Brannigan been up to when he'd swaggered up the steps to the ranch-house?

Kyle grasped at the straw of hope.

Despard cackled. It was like flint chips rattled in a tin mug.

"I ain't givin' up neither, Mr Hardy. The account ain't settled till both the big man an' his precious son is

211

stone cold dead."

He stated his intentions in a flat, unemotional monotone that made them matter-of-fact and doubly virulent. He took up the package he'd tugged from his warbag.

He looked at Kyle assessingly. "Yuh got what it takes, pard . . . I'm going forward apiece. Cover me, will yuh? If one o' them waddies shows his noggin, I'm relyin' on yuh to salivate'im afore he c'n point his iron. *Whatever happens*. Get me?"

"Hell, Despard! Yuh can't take 'em all out thataway!"

It seemed to Kyle that what the gunhawk was planning was plain suicide. The law of averages said he couldn't confront five armed men and walk back alive.

But Despard just gave his dry, death-rattle chuckle again and said, "Jest yuh watch me like I says. Thar's more ways to skin a cat . . . "

Argument was rudely curtailed by action. The man in black pushed his way forward through the underbrush on his belly. At the very edge of the copse, he paused. He took a lucifer from his coat pocket and grated it into flaring life on the sole of his boot, shielding the flame with his cupped hands.

By the match's own flicker of light, Kyle saw Despard apply it to the end of the mysterious, paper-wrapped parcel. Instantly something sputtered acridly.

With the fizzing parcel trailing white smoke, Despard burst from the cover of the silver beeches and made a weaving sprint toward the shed, zigzagging past a browsing Triple-Z cayuse that momentarily obscured him from their enemies.

Kyle thought he knew now, and his blood ran cold.

But he had his own part to play.

The brim of a hat poked round from the back of the shed. Almost automatically, he fired his Winchester. Splinters flew off the pine planks and the head abruptly withdrew.

Halfway to the shed, Despard stopped and hurled his parcel into the structure. Then he was ducking and streaking back and the horse he'd passed before broke into a spooked gallop.

From behind the shed came one hoarse bellow of alarm. For one instant in his life Bart Brannigan knew horror.

The dynamite exploded in a vivid flash of flame that seemed to engulf the shed, tearing it into a thousand flying parts. The sound deadened Kyle's ears and the ground beneath his feet quaked with the shock of it.

After that burst of appalling fury, there was a dead silence and the only moving thing where the shed had been was a rising column of black smoke from the fragmented debris scattered around a shallow, ragged-edged crater.

Despard returned to the beeches, picked up his rifle and calmly began reloading it with shells from his pockets. Next he took the worn-butted .45s from his low-slung, tied-down holsters, thumbed cartridges from the loops in his belt and slipped them into the chambers that were empty.

He said nothing; his eyes were like marble.

Kyle watched his gaunt hands working with steady, deadly purpose. There was only one Brannigan left now. Lance. And he'd gone into the ranch-house, which was the only place where Verity might be. If she was still alive.

Having witnessed the ruthless extermination of Brannigan senior and his cohorts, Kyle was disturbingly conscious that Despard wasn't going to be too fussy about who got hurt when he started slinging that lead he was packing into his hardware. He was a real ornery cuss, and then some.

"Are we aimin' to go in after that dude son o' Brannigan's?" he asked tentatively.

"Ain't nothin' else left on my agenda, *amigo*."

"The gal may be in there. We'd better go careful like," Kyle suggested.

Despard shrugged, unmoved. "She

takes her chances, I guess." He picked up the Winchester and slammed three shots into the ranch-house.

Kyle winced.

Glass tinkled. But there was no answering fire. No woman's screams. Nothing.

Despard uncoiled his long limbs and moved off down the slope and out of the copse.

Kyle strode after him, his legs stiff from crouching. They went past Tom Tyler's grave and skirted the place where the shed had been. Despard spared the spreadeagled shapes of Brannigan and his last four hirelings nothing more than a cursory glance.

Kyle swallowed. The corpses were blackened and their clothing ragged. Broken limbs had left the dead shapes irreverently contorted.

"Take it easy," Kyle warned as they stepped up, hand-guns drawn, on to the verandah. Despard's footfalls were far from noiseless on the boards.

"I'm pickin' the varmint's already lit

a shuck," Despard opined. "Slipped out some back way durin' the ruckus, the lily-livered dawg."

A quick search proved him right. A door swung open on creaking hinges at the far side of the house from the battle scene.

Kyle's heart seemed to be up in his throat. "Looks like he musta taken Miss Verity with him," he said.

"Can yuh read sign?" Despard asked.

"Like a book. I was an army scout once."

"Then let's go find our hosses."

★ ★ ★

In her room in the ranch-house Verity had heard the fresh outbreak of gunfire that signified the arrival at the Diamond-T of Kyle Hardy and Jules Despard. But she couldn't understand who was shooting at whom. Nor did she have many moments to think about it.

She heard the urgent thump of

boots in the passage outside, then the doorknob rattled and twisted before her wide-eyed gaze.

"Git this door open, gal! We know you're in there!"

It was the imperious voice of Lance Brannigan.

"Go away, you murderer!" she cried in anguish.

Lance laughed cruelly. "Not yet, pretty one. You an' me got some long unfinished business. Or should I say pleasure? So open up, or I'll smash the blasted door down!"

"You can rot in hell!"

The door was made of several panels set in a stouter frame. Contemptuously, Lance Brannigan thrust his shoulder into the panel above the knob. It gave, cracking open down the grain. Drawing his Colt, he carelessly used the handsome carved butt to hammer and split the broken pieces loose.

As he thrust his hand in to shove the jammed chair free, Verity fired her .32.

The bullet tore through the ornamental edging of Lance's buckskin shirt. He withdrew his hand rapidly with an obscene oath.

"Throw out that gun, you goddamned bitch, or it'll be the worse for you!" He backed up his demand with a random shot into the room with his .45.

A mirror shattered with an explosive crack above Verity's head. She screamed and ducked the flying shards. Then she made her mistake. Her wits stunned by the noise, she went to brush the glass from her hair, reflexively lowering both her head and the Smith and Wesson.

Before she knew it, Lance was in the room and gripping her gun wrist. "Got you!" he grunted. He wrestled her on to the bed, sticking his hard knee into her back and twisting her arm up behind her.

The pistol clattered to the floor from her suddenly nerveless fingers.

Somewhere else in the house came the sound of glass shattering, hit by a stray shot as the gunfighting outside intensified.

"I reckon it's time you an' I made tracks, precious." Lance said. "It's gettin' kinda unhealthy hereabouts."

Verity's heart leapt. She realised then that someone was firing on the Brannigans; that the attackers themselves were under attack.

But her hope was quickly all but crushed. Lance dragged her to her feet and thrust her urgently at gunpoint out of the room and on to the back porch. There was a fiendish gloating on his hot face. The unmitigated lust was written large in his pale, glittering eyes. His smile was satanically evil.

"We'll let my pa's boys take care of this can o' worms. Our settlin's gonna be done real slow an' quiet — 'cept mebbe for some gaspin' an' screamin'."

Holstering his Colt and twisting her arm up behind her, he kneed her in the back again and forced her toward the corral. It was some fifty yards from the house, heading from the corner diagonally opposite the silver beeches.

Verity went to cry out, hoping that because of a lull in the shooting the unknown persons who'd taken on the Brannigan gang might hear her woman's voice and be able to investigate.

But Lance anticipated her as she drew breath. "No you don't, bitch!" he snarled. His left hand clapped over her mouth, fingers and thumb digging deep into her cheeks, and he force-marched her on.

Along the corral fence were some pieces of rope. Lance seized one length up and threw Verity forward on to her knees, before kicking her without compunction on to her side and tying her wrists behind her. Then he whipped off his silk bandanna and tightly gagged her.

It was at this moment the dynamite blew. The racket it made was deafening. Stupefying. Afterwards there was just a long, ominous silence.

It was the sound of death.

Lance was as shocked as Verity was. Through eyes wide with fear she saw her captor whirl about and hop from one foot to another as though uncertain what to do. His surprise told her that it was not the Brannigans who'd brought the explosive here, which meant it had to be their enemies. And she exulted.

But Lance was not irresolute for long. He had the base instincts of an animal and in extremity it was these that governed him. Frightened, his reaction was to run for home. But he was cunning, too. Cussing profanely, he attached the loose ends of her bonds to the fence and ran off into the stables adjacent to the corral.

For one joyous moment, Verity thought he was going to abandon her and look out for his own skin. She saw the light of a match flare and flicker inside the shadowy building. He wasn't hiding there; what would be the point with herself left by the corral in plain view? Was he going to set the stables afire?

The questions were answered when he returned quickly with a saddle, blanket, two bridles and a lariat. The match had been for light.

From somewhere beyond the house, three rifle shots rang out. Glass smashed and Verity thought she caught a distant murmur of voices carried on the breeze.

Lance had already dropped most of his load; he'd gone inside the corral and was amid the dozen or so restive horses that milled around there. Some were galloping back and forth, but Lance succeeded in hustling two fairly quiet mares out the gate. He bridled both of them and hitched them to the fence. He threw the blanket over the chestnut. The saddle followed and he cinched it down.

That done, he freed Verity from the fence and dragged her alongside the gate. He jerked out his Colt.

"Get up on the gate and on to the bay!" he growled. "Or I'll put a bullet in each of your ankles."

223

Verity did as she was ordered. With her hands tied, she had to lean her body against the fence to steady herself as she mounted the bars. As she got to the third bar and tried to swing her leg across the mare's bare back, Lance got impatient with her slow, wobbly progress. He put his hand under her and boosted her on to the horse. She felt his fingers clutching through the whipcord pants. Verity was not only hurt physically, she was filled with revulsion. It was a sickening hint of the vile handling he had in store for her.

Once she'd forked the horse, Lance dropped the loop of the lariat over her head. He pulled the lasso till it fitted her neck like a collar, the rough rope rasping against her soft skin.

"This is the first favour you're gonna do me, Miss High-an'-Mighty Tyler," he told her with a sneer. "You're gonna guarantee me a safe ride outa here. You know how?"

She shook her head nervously.

"They call it bein' led Comanche, savvy?"

Then Verity understood. She'd heard from her father how the Comanche Indians had devised a fiendishly effective way of conducting their prisoners through hostile territory on horseback. A noose was placed about the prisoner's neck. If the prisoner tried to escape, or his mounted captor was attacked, the prisoner was jerked from his own horse by the tightening noose and dragged to his death.

She was hostage to a man as wicked as a savage red devil!

15

A Killer's Last Shot

THE sky was clear and cloudless and stars as big as silver dollars were bright enough to make shadows.

Kyle Hardy had cast around the Diamond-T home-lot, using up several begrudged minutes, till he found two sets of fresh tracks leaving to the north by a little-used bridle-path.

He had no doubt then that Lance Brannigan had ridden off with Verity Tyler.

"But these tracks don't seem to indicate any big hurry," he commented. His craggy brows were lowered in a frown of puzzlement.

"Mebbe he was wounded," Despard offered dispassionately. He moved his rangy horse into a steady hand-canter alongside Kyle.

Kyle grunted. "Naw . . . I only got the one shot at him and he jumped into the house like a scalded cat. An' I reckon he's taken the gal with him. Now why would he'of done that?"

"A gal ain't gonna be much good to him where he's agoin'." Despard chuckled maliciously. "That two-timer's bound fer Hell if'n I have t' follow him to the end o'the world!"

The path climbed, leading out of the valley to a pass through the mountains. They were forced into single file and a walking pace as thick brush crowded in. The grey-green foliage was shoulder-high in places and could easily have swallowed up a rider. But there was no sign of any broken or trampled branches.

Kyle thought aloud. "He can't know his father's dead. Not for sure. I reckon he'll head for home and reinforcements, goin' by some roundabout route to shake off pursuit."

"Or t' ambush it," Despard said dryly.

It was an eventuality they'd both been alive to from the outset. They kept an unbroken look-out during their slow progress. Their eyes swept the ridge tops continuously for any giveaway movements.

Another worry on Kyle's mind was the manner and morals of his unorthodox ally. When it came to the showdown, he didn't doubt Despard would blast away at Lance Brannigan without mercy — or any consideration for the young hellion's hostage. He'd seen ample evidence of Despard's total ruthlessness. The thought of Verity being caught in a vicious crossfire made him break out in a cold sweat.

He tried to broach the subject. "We can't do anythin' too rash lest it'll endanger the gal," he suggested.

Despard was dismissive. "Ain't no one gonna hogtie Jules Despard, mister," he said flatly.

Kyle forced himself to remember that the man he rode with had his own black-hearted agenda. He could be trusted to do only one thing — serve his own interests. He'd freed him, Hardy, from the Sweetwater Springs calaboose solely because he needed an extra gunhand and no other than himself seemed to be available.

He recalled how he'd shot down young Tom Tyler for no other reason than the promise of *dinero*. He wondered how many more tenderfeet and fools lay scattered down the bloody trail of his nefarious past.

His present interest was revenge on the Brannigans. He wouldn't be satisfied until he'd wiped the double-crossing, two-timing range dude who'd cheated him off the face of the Earth. And nothing was going to be allowed to get in his way.

Kyle determined that if Verity was at threat from his activities, he would intervene. He would kill Despard if it came to it, regardless of any debt he owed him. But he would have to be very wary.

For three hours they rode, till the sky was greying in the east. Despard's right hand rested permanently on a Colt butt. Kyle wondered how it wasn't cramped into a fixed claw. After the exchange about Verity, they spoke rarely, and then only in low mutters that wouldn't carry and about details of the signs they followed.

Then Despard's streaky dun nickered, its nostrils slightly flaring. The gun-slick put his hand to its muzzle.

"Listen," he grated in a whisper. "The hoss has sensed somethin'."

Kyle was cupping a hand behind his ear when a sharp crack rang out, seemingly from somewhere above them, which was entirely possible, since they were ascending through a steep-sided, winding defile that looked as though it would give eventual access to the mesa high to their left.

At the sound of the single gunshot,

both riders whirled around, Colts drawn. But they saw nothing.

Despard swore.

A mocking laugh rang out. "I know yo're down there, whoever you might be. I can't see you and you can't see me. But I can hear you comin'. Well, keep on real slow, 'cause I wanna see who you are an' I got somethin' for you to see that might make you change your minds about followin' me."

"It's Brannigan right enough," Kyle hissed through clenched teeth. "What do we do?"

"We surely go on, pard," Despard decreed.

Kyle thumbed back the hammer of his .45.

As though he might have heard the small sound, Brannigan called out from his hidden position, "Don't anybody creep up on me with trigger-happy delusions. They do an' Verity Tyler will be dead."

The threat crystallised Kyle's greatest fear. He would kill Verity. From the menace in his voice, Kyle knew he meant it.

"Take it easy, Despard," he warned in a whisper, reluctantly lowering the gun's hammer and sheathing it.

But the gunman merely lifted the shoulders of his black coat in a kind of shrug, holstered his Colt and kneed the dun forward.

They rode up and out on to the mesa, Despard in the lead. The wind met their faces — Kyle's set and grim; Despard's just its usual expressionless mask with slit eyes and slit mouth.

And Kyle froze when he saw the tableau set amidst the rough, knee-high yellow grass.

Lance Brannigan sat a chestnut mare. A lead rein stretched to a bay mare mounted by Verity. But it wasn't only the lead rein that linked the pair. A rope noose around Verity's neck had its other end looped around Brannigan's saddle horn.

Kyle cottoned on instantly. If Brannigan let go the lead rein, and

232

his horse was spurred away, Verity would be dismounted and her neck probably snapped as surely as by any hangman. If by any chance she was not killed instantly, she would be dragged to her death by a careering horse.

But Brannigan, too, was dealt a shock.

Despard, he'd assumed, had been sent packing by his father with a flea in his ear; Hardy he'd supposed to be in jail, awaiting trial for the murder of Maria Cortazzi.

Yet this presumably was the pair who'd fired on the Triple-Z crowd when they'd stormed the Tyler ranch!

His momentary astonishment was all the chance Despard considered he needed. His right-hand Colt slid from greased leather like lightning.

In the split-second before he triggered, Kyle also was drawing, the blood running icily in his veins instantly thawed.

He'd read Despard's cold mind.

Or he thought he had.

They fired in near unison. The second shot, though scarcely aimed, slammed into Despard's gaunt torso, crashing him from the saddle. But Kyle knew as the slug left his Colt that he had been too late to stop the gun-slick firing — and that Verity was therefore as good as dead.

"You bastard!" he cried.

But it was the first shot — Despard's — that was the stunner.

It sliced across the horsehair rope midway between Brannigan's saddle and Verity's neck. And the frayed strands parted as the two mares became abruptly and understandably skittish!

Before Kyle could even appreciate the astounding thing that had happened, he was having to fire again: Lance Brannigan, though startled out of his wits by his opponents' staggering nerve, had drawn his own fancy Colts and was trying to take aim as his horse pranced.

His face was demoniacal in its fury. His scheme had been thwarted!

He loosed off two wild shots before something hit him, hard, and his innards became a cauldron of pain that sent roaring messages that blackened his brain and toppled him sightless to the hard ground.

But when he died there seconds after, his pale eyes were still open in a blank stare of stupid surprise.

Kyle jumped from the saddle uncertain whom he should run to first. He chose Despard.

Blood was making pink the spittle that foamed from his thin lips. "Fine pard'ner yuh was," he rasped horribly. Then he slumped back and was dead.

Whether the gunfighter had been aiming to kill Lance Brannigan with his last shot, or whether he'd severed the rope deliberately rather than by freakish chance, Kyle Hardy would never know.

★ ★ ★

Several days later, Verity Tyler and Kyle Hardy sat in the two rawhide chairs on the front verandah of the Diamond-T. Debris and damage from the Brannigans' assault was still much in evidence and there was a second fresh grave out by the silver beeches.

Something — was it just the majestic sweep of the scene beneath the cerulean sky? — seemed to cast an awesome spell over them both.

A lot of work had still to be done, and many questions had still to be answered. But Sweetwater folk free from the shadow of their oppressors had already been pledging their help to Verity to get the Diamond-T up and running again, if that was what she wanted.

Alternatively, it was suggested a fair price would be bid at auction . . .

Kyle's plans were no more clear-cut. Though for him, that was typical. He'd travelled many miles and seen a lot in his thirty-some years. Now it included a full-blown range war. But it was all over and he was exactly where he'd started, owning next to nothing, having no roots anywhere.

Verity said slowly, as though to correct something in her mind, "So you didn't come to Sweetwater Valley accidentally?"

"Nope. An' I sure hope you won't think I was deceivin' in not sayin' so right off. That was truly not my intention. Events kinda pushed explanations aside."

"It was the military who sent you here?" Verity prompted.

"It was. I was once an army scout, you see, an' I was at a loose end when they up and offered me a special assignment. Seein's how I weren't doin' anythin' more worthwhile, I accepted. The Apache Indians had made claims that warrin' white men in Sweetwater Valley were tryin' to discredit them with false words about the murder of a family of ranchers."

"The Paynters."

"That was the name. The Apaches' evidence included the stub of a distinctive black cheroot. Later, from somethin'

Jules Despard let slip and I've now followed up, it appeared this brand was used by the Brannigans. So I guess they were the culprits in the raid on the Paynters, and the Apache tribe is cleared."

"And your work here is over." Verity sighed. "While mine is just beginning. I guess you'll be moving on, taking on more undercover work from the military perhaps."

"That ain't necessarily so," Kyle said, his grey eyes serious. "These last few days I've been dreamin' of gettin' me a nice little job on a nice little ranch. An' it seems to me stayin' on the Diamond-T payroll is jest the way to go about it."

A slow smile touched Verity's trembling lips. She was agreeably surprised that he might want to settle down. She'd always thought of him as a wanderer, footloose and fancy-free, belonging nowhere.

"You'll be more than welcome," she said.

When her grieving for her brother and father was over, who knew what the future might hold?

THE END

Other titles in the Linford Western Library:

TOP HAND
Wade Everett

The Broken T was big. But no ranch is big enough to let a man hide from himself.

GUN WOLVES OF LOBO BASIN
Lee Floren

The Feud was a blood debt. When Smoke Talbot found the outlaws who gunned down his folks he aimed to nail their hide to the barn door.

SHOTGUN SHARKEY
Marshall Grover

The westbound coach carrying the indomitable Larry and Stretch headed for a shooting showdown.

FARGO: PANAMA GOLD
John Benteen

With foreign money behind him, Buckner was going to destroy the Panama Canal before it could be completed. Fargo's job was to stop Buckner.

FARGO: THE SHARPSHOOTERS
John Benteen

The Canfield clan, thirty strong were raising hell in Texas. Fargo was tough enough to hold his own against the whole clan.

PISTOL LAW
Paul Evan Lehman

Lance Jones came back to Mustang for just one thing — revenge! Revenge on the people who had him thrown in jail.

FARGO: MASSACRE RIVER
John Benteen

The ambushers up ahead had now blocked the road. Fargo's convoy was a jumble, a perfect target for the insurgents' weapons!

SUNDANCE: DEATH IN THE LAVA
John Benteen

The Modoc's captured the wagon train and its cargo of gold. But now the halfbreed they called Sundance was going after it . . .

HARSH RECKONING
Phil Ketchum

Five years of keeping himself alive in a brutal prison had made Brand tough and careless about who he gunned down . . .

SUNDANCE: SILENT ENEMY
John Benteen

A lone crazed Cheyenne was on a personal war path. They needed to pit one man against one crazed Indian. That man was Sundance.

LASSITER
Jack Slade

Lassiter wasn't the kind of man to listen to reason. Cross him once and he'll hold a grudge for years to come — if he let you live that long.

LAST STAGE TO GOMORRAH
Barry Cord

Jeff Carter, tough ex-riverboat gambler, now had himself a horse ranch that kept him free from gunfights and card games. Until Sturvesant of Wells Fargo showed up.

McALLISTER ON THE COMANCHE CROSSING
Matt Chisholm

The Comanche, McAllister owes them a life — and the trail is soaked with the blood of the men who had tried to outrun them before.

QUICK-TRIGGER COUNTRY
Clem Colt

Turkey Red hooked up with Curly Bill Graham's outlaw crew. But wholesale murder was out of Turk's line, so when range war flared he bucked the whole border gang alone . . .

CAMPAIGNING
Jim Miller

Ambushed on the Santa Fe trail, Sean Callahan is saved by two Indian strangers. But there'll be more lead and arrows flying before the band join Kit Carson against the Comanches.

GUNSLINGER'S RANGE
Jackson Cole

Three escaped convicts are out for revenge. They won't rest until they put a bullet through the head of the dirty snake who locked them behind bars.

RUSTLER'S TRAIL
Lee Floren

Jim Carlin knew he would have to stand up and fight because he had staked his claim right in the middle of Big Ike Outland's best grass.

THE TRUTH ABOUT SNAKE RIDGE
Marshall Grover

The troubleshooters came to San Cristobal to help the needy. For Larry and Stretch the turmoil began with a brawl and then an ambush.

WOLF DOG RANGE
Lee Floren

Will Ardery would stop at nothing, unless something stopped him first — like a bullet from Pete Manly's gun.

DEVIL'S DINERO
Marshall Grover

Plagued by remorse, a rich old reprobate hired the Texas Troubleshooters to deliver a fortune in greenbacks to each of his victims.

GUNS OF FURY
Ernest Haycox

Dane Starr, alias Dan Smith, wanted to close the door on his past and hang up his guns, but people wouldn't let him.

FIGHTING RAMROD
Charles N. Heckelmann

Most men would have cut their losses, but Frazer counted the bullets in his guns and said he'd soak the range in blood before he'd give up another inch of what was his.

LONE GUN
Eric Allen

Smoke Blackbird had been away too long. The Lequires had seized the Blackbird farm, forcing the Indians and settlers off, and no one seemed willing to fight! He had to fight alone.

THE THIRD RIDER
Barry Cord

Mel Rawlins wasn't going to let anything stand in his way. His father was murdered, his two brothers gone. Now Mel rode for vengeance.

HELL RIDERS
Steve Mensing

Wade Walker's kid brother, Duane, was locked up in the Silver City jail facing a rope at dawn. Wade was a ruthless outlaw, but he was smart, and he had vowed to have his brother out of jail before morning!

DESERT OF THE DAMNED
Nelson Nye

The law was after him for the murder of a marshal — a murder he didn't commit. Breen was after him for revenge — and Breen wouldn't stop at anything . . . blackmail, a frameup . . . or murder.

DAY OF THE COMANCHEROS
Steven C. Lawrence

Their very name struck terror into men's hearts — the Comancheros, a savage army of cutthroats who swept across Texas, leaving behind a bloodstained trail of robbery and murder.

BRETT RANDALL, GAMBLER
E. B. Mann

Larry Day had the choice of running away from the law or of assuming a dead man's place. No matter what he decided he was bound to end up dead.

THE GUNSHARP
William R. Cox

The Eggerleys weren't very smart. They trained their sights on Will Carney and Arizona's biggest blood bath began.

THE DEPUTY OF SAN RIANO
Lawrence A. Keating and
Al. P. Nelson

When a man fell dead from his horse, Ed Grant was spotted riding away from the scene. The deputy sheriff rode out after him and came up against everything from gunfire to dynamite.

ARIZONA DRIFTERS
W. C. Tuttle

When drifting Dutton and Lonnie Steelman decide to become partners they find that they have a common enemy in the formidable Thurston brothers.

TOMBSTONE
Matt Braun

Wells Fargo paid Luke Starbuck to outgun the silver-thieving stagecoach gang at Tombstone. Before long Luke can see the only thing bearing fruit in this eldorado will be the gallows tree.

HIGH BORDER RIDERS
Lee Floren

Buckshot McKee and Tortilla Joe cut the trail of a border tough who was running Mexican beef into Texas. They stopped the smuggler in his tracks.